### 'You're beautiful, Kit...'

Nobody had ever called her beautiful before.

'Don't let's waste time talking.'

After a long minute Brook's hands clamped hard on her shoulders, and put her away from him.

'Get below,' he ordered her roughly, 'while I've still got the strength to let you go.'

Kit stared up at him bewilderedly. Like a child, she did not want this one perfect day to end.

'If you make me go, I'll hate you.'

'I must.'

**Dear Reader**

The summer holidays are now behind us — but Mills & Boon still have lots of treats in store for you! Why not indulge yourself in long, romantic evenings by the fire? We're sure you'll find our heroes simply irresistible! And perhaps you'd like to experience the exotic beauty of the Bahamas — or the glamour of Milan? Whatever you fancy, just curl up with this month's selection of enchanting love stories — and let your favourite authors carry you away!

Happy reading!

*The Editor*

**Sue Peters** was born and brought up in Warwickshire, where she still lives. Her hobbies are writing, gardening, walking and music. She joined the family of Mills & Boon writers via one of their 'Write a Romance' competitions, and with their initial encouragement found herself launched on a new career, although her love of writing is such that it will always remain first and foremost her most pleasurable hobby. In spite of writing romances, she remains contentedly single!

# TOMORROW'S MAN

BY

## SUE PETERS

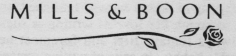

# MILLS & BOON

MILLS & BOON LIMITED
ETON HOUSE, 18-24 PARADISE ROAD
RICHMOND, SURREY TW9 1SR

First published in Great Britain in 1993
by Mills & Boon Limited

© Sue Peters 1993

Australian copyright 1993
Philippine copyright 1993
This edition 1993

ISBN 0 263 78041 4

Set in Times Roman 12 on 12 pt
01-9311-39862 C

Made and printed in Great Britain

# CHAPTER ONE

'A TABLE for two, madam?'

'A table for one, please.'

She tried to make her voice sound brisk, confident, uncaring. Instead, as usual, it came out sounding defensive. She wished she had carried on driving, not bothering to eat until she finally arrived home.

Would she ever get used to it? Kit wondered bleakly.

Would she ever learn not to cringe away from the cool assessment in the eyes of waiters and their like, whose guarded stare wondered why this girl, with the unhappy hazel eyes, should ask for a table for one?

Kit's fingers came up in an unconscious, nervous gesture, pushing back the straight shining curtain of her shoulder-length bob, tucking it firmly behind her right ear. It would not stay here for long. It never did. The silky brown-gold strands had a will of their own. But for the moment it kept them from falling across her face.

'A table for one, please.'

This time it sounded firmer, more assured. Kit congratulated herself. A good stout shell could hide a lack of confidence, given enough practice. It could even hide the devastating aftermath of that tragic night when details had begun to emerge from the police enquiries as to exactly where her husband had been going on his last, fateful journey, which had ended when his high-powered sports car, driven too fast as usual—Paul always drove, as he lived, in the fast lane—had landed upside-down on the hard shoulder of the motorway.

Would she ever recover from the shock of learning where Paul had been going that night, and of the woman he had been going to see?

Over a year later, it still haunted her.

For her sanity's sake, Kit had struggled to come to terms with the pain, but the humiliation was something else, made worse by detailed reporting of every sordid detail in the local newspaper.

In self-defence, Kit had grown a shell, but underneath she knew herself to be still vulnerable. The experience bit deeply into her confidence, corrosive, like acid.

'Madam?'

Confused, she dragged herself back to her surroundings. The waiter was regarding her strangely, evidently expecting an answer to a question she had been too absorbed in her own thoughts to hear.

Kit stammered, 'I—I'm sorry. I didn't quite catch . . . ?'

'Will this table be suitable, madam?'

'Yes. Oh, yes, thank you. It will do nicely.'

It was one of two small tables, placed close together, and tucked out of sight behind a potted palm. As if being alone made you somehow dangerous. Someone people wanted to put out of sight, and forget. A man was already seated at one table, engaged with his meal. The waiter led Kit towards the other, and politely pulled out a chair for her.

She hesitated. If she took the chair offered, she would be obliged to sit facing the man at the other table. She would have much preferred to sit the other way, with her back turned towards him, shutting him out.

But if she took the other chair instead it would seem like a snub to the waiter, and an insult to the other diner. With a mental shrug she summoned a passable smile for the waiter, and sat down on the chair he offered, first carefully propping her bulky portfolio against the potted palm. It was large, and awkward to carry for someone of her diminutive height, but its contents represented too much hard work for her to risk leaving it, even in a locked car.

'Thank you.' She gave a cursory glance at the menu which the waiter held out for her to see, and decided, 'Soup, please.'

'And...?' The man waited expectantly, pencil poised.

'Oh—er—an omelette, I think, and coffee.'

She did not care what it was she ate, so long as it gave her sufficient energy to finish her journey, and get home. She had to have fuel, as well as her car, if she was to drive any further that day.

The soup tasted of nothing when it came, Kit's lack of interest in the chef's rich creation a reproach echoed by her too-slender figure, which betrayed far too many similar, hasty snacks, eaten from sheer necessity, and not for any pleasure in the food.

Strange, that, because at one time she had prided herself on her culinary skills. Although their flat was not large, she and Paul had entertained a great deal. Looking back, Kit realised that it was Paul who had done the entertaining, while she herself had done the work.

Hindsight gave you crystal-clear vision, she discovered wryly. It dispelled the rosy illusions, and the harsh light of reality disposed of the myth of what she had innocently believed to be love. Would that it could also cure the hurt. Kit crumbled her bread roll in tense fingers, and became aware that the man at the other table was looking in her direction.

Thinking she might be an easy pick-up?

Men had it all, she thought bitterly. No one questioned a man being on his own. A woman on her own was immediately suspect.

'If you are not using your salt, may I borrow it? I don't seem to have any on my table.'

'I don't use it.'

'In that case...'

He half rose from his seat, and reached across and annexed the salt cellar in long, slender fingers. He did not need to reach out far with his arm. His considerable height made anything more than restricted movement unnecessary in order to capture the desired object.

Automatically, Kit's artist's eye registered detail. A fastidiously manicured hand. A snowy cuff under a perfectly tailored jacket sleeve. Expensive cuff-links. Not like the flamboyant creations which Paul had favoured. These had the classic touch of exclusivity, neat discs relieved only by the beautifully engraved outline of a leaping dolphin on each one.

Kit wondered idly if the dolphin had any significance.

'Thank you. I'll keep it, if you don't want it.'

Kit's eyes flew to his face. Absorbed in the dolphin, she had momentarily forgotten the salt cellar.

'Feel free.' Her tone discouraged any attempt at further conversation.

With a jaw that firm, and lips to match, this man would feel free to do whatever he chose, without asking anyone's permission, she opined. His lower lip had a fullness which betrayed a lurking sensuality, but the steel-grey glance held an iron control, which would harness any such emotions to his will.

Tall, dark, and handsome, she jeered silently at the face which loomed, briefly, above her own. It was a strong face. An interesting one, from an artist's point of view, but she was in the business of illustrating books and their jackets, not portrait painting.

If she had wanted to paint a portrait, she would not choose her fellow diner as a sitter, she decided. She felt, uneasily, that it would be he, and not the artist, who would dictate what the finished canvas must look like.

She would not choose a man as a subject, anyway. She had finished with men.

So she could not believe the flash of pique which assailed her, when he transferred the salt cellar to his own table, used its contents sparingly, and resumed eating without another glance in her direction. The shell which she had cultivated since Paul was not so impregnable as she had led herself to believe.

You should know better! she derided herself. The solitary stranger had more than his fair share of good looks. But so had Paul, and see where those had led to.

Kit scarcely tasted the fresh young vegetables, and the mouth-watering fluffiness of her omelette. She ate mechanically, and reached for her coffee when she had finished with the feeling of relief which ended all of her meals these days.

Eating gave her unwanted time in which to think. It was much easier, and far less painful, to work. Work occupied her mind to the exclusion of bitter memories. She would finish her coffee, and go on her way, if possible before the man at the next table, who had reached the coffee stage too, she noticed.

She shrank from emerging from the restaurant as a twosome, perhaps walking to the parking slots together, exchanging banalities, as strangers did. Even such slight contact was sufficient to raise her hackles, since Paul.

She would be glad to reach home, and shut herself away from the world for a few hours. Maggie, her next-flat-neighbour, would most likely drop in for a coffee and a chat later on.

She usually did, when Kit returned after a few days' absence, and her cheerful chatter would keep thoughts at bay until bedtime.

*Crash*!

The rending sound of metal-to-metal impact brought diners to their feet. The tinkle of shattered glass echoed through a brief, shocked silence, and then everybody started to talk at once.

'Somebody's car is a write-off,' the man at the next table remarked coolly, and rose too, leaving his coffee unfinished as he made for the door with long strides, doubtless to find out if his own car was involved.

With those sort of cuff-links at his sleeve-ends, he probably did not need to worry over-much about the financial implications of such a disaster, which no doubt accounted for his calmness, Kit reflected. She felt just the reverse, herself. She grabbed her portfolio, and hurried in his wake. Reputedly, trouble never came by halves, and she had an awful premonition...

'My car's intact.' The man stopped at the entrance steps to survey the parking slots. Trotting at speed behind him, Kit collided with his back, unable to stop herself in time.

'I'm so sorry, I...'

It was like hitting rock. The stranger remained immovable, while Kit shook with the impact. He remarked, as if he had not noticed the collision, 'It looks as if that little red Metro has caught the full force. I wonder who it belongs to?'

Kit had an overwhelming feeling that the man with the dolphin cuff-links already knew, but since an answer seemed to be called for she told him anyway. 'It's mine,' she said faintly.

She stared in disbelief at the wreckage of her vital means of transport, without which it would be impossible to fit in all the work which the publishers demanded of her, and which was rapidly making her name as an illustrator.

Her portfolio, essential to keep her sketches and paintings flat, was half as high as she was, and, on her current measurements, about three times as wide. Lugging it across country on crowded trains and buses presented awesome difficulties. If it got bent, sat upon, or otherwise squashed, it would hazard her many hours of painstaking work inside.

She still had roughly sixty miles to travel in order to reach the publishers with her present offering. How much would taxi fares cost for such a distance? she wondered. Even supposing a cab would be willing to make such a long journey. Her mind boggled. The figure would probably go right off the meter.

But she had promised to get her sketches into the editor's hands today, in order to meet a printing deadline.

A distressed voice cut into her jumbled thoughts. It rose high and panicky above the excited chatter of the diners and restaurant staff, who had all crowded out to see what had happened.

'It wasn't my fault. This little lad, he ran across the road after his ball. I had to either hit him, or hit the car.'

He was only a youth. A delivery driver, probably in his first job, and with the front of his van hopelessly embedded in the crumpled rear of her savaged Metro. Kit's naturally warm heart made her temporarily forget her antipathy towards men. She stepped towards the youth impulsively.

'If that's what happened, no one will blame you for it.'

The van driver's shocked white face turned towards her. He looked ready to burst into tears. 'The owner of this car will.'

'I'm the owner of this car. Or what's left of it.' Resolutely Kit dragged her eyes away from the mangled metal. She had survived worse.

Losing a man was capable of inflicting worse hurt than losing a Metro.

'Just think how much worse it would have been, if it had done that sort of damage to the child,' she urged.

'I swerved automatically, to miss him.'

'Did you?'

'Did I what?'

'Miss him?'

'Yes, thank goodness. The little demon ran away laughing.'

'Then be thankful that only the vehicles are damaged. They can easily be repaired.'

People could not. Neither their bodies, nor their hearts. Kit became aware of a newly familiar deep voice, applauding in her ear, 'Nobly said.'

The man with the dolphin cuff-links stood at her shoulder. Jeering at her?

Kit's lips tightened. With difficulty, she ignored him, helped by the timely arrival of a panda car, which ejected its crew to take charge. One of the officers drew out the inevitable notebook. 'Did anyone witness the accident?'

'I did.' A traffic warden came to the fore, and proceeded to shoot down the evil reputation of her profession in the eyes of the motoring public by standing up for the young van driver.

'He is quite correct in what he said. His quick thinking saved that child's life. I was on the other side of the road, and saw it happen. The driver had no chance to miss the car.'

'Whose car...?'

'It's mine,' Kit admitted ruefully. 'I'll have to get someone to tow it away.'

'We'll raise them for you on our radio, miss.'

It was all over in a hectic half-hour. Kit recovered her belongings from the glove-box of the car, said a mental farewell to her sturdy little companion of many miles as the breakdown truck bore it away, and then stood forlornly on the forecourt of the restaurant, wondering what to do next.

The diners returned to their neglected lunches, and the restaurant staff to their duties, all except the waiter who had served her, and the man at the next table. The waiter offered helpfully, 'Would you like me to call a taxi for you, miss?'

'I'm not quite sure what to do. I've got to get to London somehow,' Kit answered him doubtfully.

Her doubt lay in the realisation that she had probably not got enough ready cash on her to pay for the journey. Did taxi drivers accept credit cards? The last thing she felt capable of, right now, was a hassle with an angry cab driver.

'Whereabouts in town are you heading for?' Her fellow diner joined in the conversation, and Kit answered him without thinking,

'The West End.'

It was not his business, so why did he butt in? The authoritative type, obviously. Accustomed to taking control in whatever situation he found himself—or fancied interfering in. She felt vexed with herself for having answered him, but it was too late now.

He said, 'I've got an appointment at Claridge's. It's in the area.' He crooked his arm, sliding back his immaculate shirt cuff in one economical movement, to just the right distance to enable him to consult his wristwatch.

Thin, gold, and as expensive as his cuff-links, Kit observed.

'I'll drop you off,' he decided.

Before Kit could make a move to forestall him, he reached down and coolly annexed her portfolio, and transferred it to the boot of a sleek silver-grey Jaguar that was parked in the slot next to the one where her own ill-fated Metro had met its end.

His car was, indeed, unscratched, just as he had said. Kit's first, startled thought was, His vehicle matches his eyes. The next indignant follow-up was, How dare he?

The cheek of the man, to calmly take charge in this high-handed manner. Knights in shining armour were all very well in folklore, which was where they belonged. So far as Kit was concerned, the armour was tarnished, and had no further place in her life. She spluttered, 'No, I ... you ...'

The man ignored her protest as if she had not spoken, and the waiter was of no help. He completely misunderstood her dismay, and assured her, *sotto voce*, 'You need have no fears about accepting a lift from this gentleman, miss. He's well-known to us here.'

Kit had no intention of accepting a lift, whether the man was a gentleman or otherwise, so the question of her personal safety did not arise. But, if she refused, how was she to get her sketches to the editor in time?

Her case had already disappeared into the cavernous boot of the Jaguar. She had the desperate feeling that, willy-nilly, its owner might pick her up and toss her after it. The emphatic thud of the boot lid shook her into speech, and desperately she stalled for time.

'I've still got to pay for my lunch.'

The waiter smiled. 'The gentleman paid for you both, miss.'

That settled it! Kit's lips thinned into a determined line. She was not prepared to accept those kind of favours from the stranger, no matter what her predicament. In spite of the waiter's assurance, the man might want favours in return. If he did, he was in for a nasty shock.

She marched over to where he stood, holding open his car door on the passenger side, as if expecting her to meekly embark, merely because he said so.

She told him stiffly, 'I pay for my own lunches.'

'I never accept money from a lady.'

Stalemate!

Their glances clashed, and in the grey was a hint of lurking amusement which nettled Kit still further. She tugged angrily at the zip of her shoulder-bag to reach her purse. Murphy's law prevailed, and the zip, which had never caused trouble before, refused to budge, frustrating her bid for independence. The amusement flared brighter, no longer disguised, and it echoed in his voice as he told her, 'You really won't need your purse. I've tipped the waiter, too.'

He cupped her elbow with firm fingers, and inserted Kit into the front seat of his car with a movement so deft that she found herself installed before she was able to give any further voice to her objections. Before she could raise it again he silenced her with, 'I imagine seat-belts work pretty much the same in all cars, but just in case...'

He leaned down, and across her, manipulating the belt, and the movement brought his face disconcertingly close to her own. Kit shrank back, away from him, and for a moment the stranger paused in his coupling of the belt to its waiting lock.

Her heart began to beat uncomfortably fast. She had not allowed a man to come so close to her since Paul. She had not *allowed* this one. She had simply not been able to prevent him. Her breath came fast, and a sense of panic began to take over. She longed to cry out, to thrust out her hands and push him away from her. To jump out of the car and run, regardless of her precious portfolio.

She gritted her teeth until her jaws ached, battling for self-control. Expensive aftershave teased her nostrils, arousing sensations that she had hoped were buried with Paul, and now knew that she had hoped in vain, counting seconds which seemed like hours before the lock clicked into place, and the stranger straightened away from her, and remarked, 'You'll be

in town quicker than if you had taken a cab,
so all isn't lost, after all.'

Only her beloved little Metro, and, just now,
very nearly, her self-control. The panic subsided a little as he shut the door, not seeming
to expect a reply, and Kit took several deep
breaths to try to steady her heartbeat to a more
comfortable speed, only to feel it accelerate
again as he slid into the driver's seat beside her,
and keyed the engine into softly purring life.

The seat engulfed her. Kit thought longingly
of the friendly cushion which she used to raise
her height in the Metro, and wished unavailingly that she had rescued it along with the rest
of her personal belongings. Her head only just
reached up to the stranger's shoulder. She
slanted a cautious upwards look at the clean-
cut profile above her, and pulled her eyes away
hurriedly when they met cool grey, looking
down at her.

'Comfortable?' he enquired.

'Very, thank you.'

The interior of his car was luxurious.
Physically, she was very comfortable indeed.
Mentally, she felt anything but. The Jaguar's
owner exuded a magnetic attraction. It challenged the strength of the armour which Kit
had built around herself, unerringly seeking out

unsuspected chinks, and penetrating them with the persistence of bright sunlight.

Like sunlight, Kit sensed uneasily that too much exposure could hold hidden dangers, and she felt thankful that the journey into town was no longer than sixty miles. Under his expert guidance, the smooth speed of the car ate up effortless distance.

The stranger was a superb driver, she acknowledged reluctantly. He sat in his seat as relaxed as a large jungle cat, but, like the wild creature whose namesake he drove, he remained all the while keenly alert to every slight manoeuvre of other road users, to guide his vehicle safely through the motorway mêlée.

In half the time it would have taken Kit to drive her Metro the same distance, the first evidence of the approach to London began to drift past the windows, and her companion roused her from her thoughts with an unexpected, 'You haven't told me your name yet.'

It was the first time he had spoken since leaving the restaurant, and, as a seasoned driver herself, Kit respected his silence. There were more than enough hazards on the motorway without adding a chattering passenger. She answered him briefly, 'Kit Fielding.'

She no longer used her married name. It had been easy to drop being Mrs Venables, because she was known professionally by her maiden name. She had counted herself lucky that she had her work to turn to, when Paul's affairs were finally settled.

*Affairs!* Her lips twisted. It was a sick joke, and she did not feel like laughing, either then or now. By the time the local newspaper gossip columnist had finished digging in the mud, he had unearthed more than one.

Which probably accounted for the fact that, in spite of his high salary, Paul had virtually nothing left in his bank account when he died, and there were a goodly number of unpaid bills for extravagant luxuries which Kit settled with silent resentment, knowing now who the recipients of those luxuries must be.

She thrust the memories away from her as the Jaguar executed a neat diversion round a rumbling container lorry, and her companion enquired, 'Are you by any chance Kit Fielding the illustrator?'

Fame at last! Her name had reached the ears of the mighty! Kit wondered what the stranger did. Had he any connection with the art world? He looked wealthy enough to be a collector, but that would put him out of her own orbit, if he was. Her work did not yet aspire to such heady heights. It was commercial, rather than collectable.

'I am,' she admitted crisply, despising herself for an inward rush of pleasure. She was already recognised as a foremost illustrator in her own world, but it was an undeniable boost to her ego to be recognised outside of it.

'Strange. I always imagined Kit Fielding to be a man.'

His cool rebuff returned Kit's ego's thermometer to its normal minus reading, where it had remained consistently since Paul, and the jolt of the sudden descent showed in her sharp retort.

'There's nothing strange about it. Successful artists aren't necessarily always men.'

'It's your own fault. Kit is short for Christopher.'

The arrogance of the man! He had the nerve to blame her for his own misunderstanding! Kit flashed back, 'Men don't hold the monopoly of names, either. It's also short for Christine.'

This was the second time in less than two hours that they had crossed swords, and Kit had a nasty feeling that she was coming off second best in this encounter, too. Unmoved by her thrust, her companion ignored the challenge in her tone, and remarked mildly, 'I'll be able to drop you off practically on the doorstep of Bolton House, so you won't have far to carry your portfolio. I imagine a thing of that size must make awkward luggage for someone of your height. It would flap about in a wind.'

Kit's eyes widened. The man was gifted with second sight. He not only knew all about flappy portfolios, he knew who her publishers were, as well. She should have said, 'Thank you,' but all that came out was a dazed, 'How did you . . . ?'

'Bolton House *is* where you're heading for, isn't it?'

'Yes, but . . .'

'In that case, I'll drop you off on the corner here. You should get top marks for arriving early.'

His amused tone mocked her, treating her like a child. Or patronising her, because she was a woman? Kit gritted her teeth, and had to unlock them to allow the obligatory, 'Thank you for the lift,' to emerge minutes later when he rescued her portfolio from the boot of the Jaguar, and handed it over to her with the equally obligatory,

'My pleasure.'

The taunting look in his eyes made Kit wonder guiltily if the journey had been a pleasure for him. He must have found her a prickly passenger. But if not they were even, she salved her conscience, edgily aware of his eyes following her every step as she walked away from him towards the familiar portico of Bolton House.

His searching look pursued her. She felt a compelling urge to run and hide herself behind one of the friendly pillars, and only restrained herself with difficulty. A stiff breeze blew along the street, straight into her face, flapping her portfolio against her legs and making it difficult for her to walk in a straight line. She struggled to control its sail-like antics, cursing its awkwardness which made a dignified retreat impossible, and hating the stranger's mocking witness of her difficulty.

If only she were several inches taller, of model height, with a patrician nose which she could look down, she wished not for the first time. Her own pert, uptilted member was useless as an aid to dignity, and she gained the steps of Bolton House with a sigh of relief. Safe at last behind one of the entrance pillars, she risked a peep back along the street, and mortification flooded her.

The Jaguar and its owner were gone.

So powerful had been the impact of the man that Kit had felt the force of his presence, even when he was no longer there.

The feeling of pique returned, because he had not waited to see her safely to her destination, admittedly only yards away from where he had dropped her. She thrust aside the feeling angrily. She had not expected him to wait, had not wanted him to. And, because he had not, she felt somehow diminished.

The old familiar depression set in as she made her way to the lift. Why should he wait, when he had an appointment at Claridge's? She wondered idly whom it was with. It was easy to imagine such a man meeting a woman with the elegant height which she, Kit, so envied. Perhaps a beautifully dressed sophisticate, from the same wealthy world as himself. Her own tailored travelling costume, of fine wool, and of the same soft golden-brown as her hair, seemed suddenly uninspired as Kit pressed the button to the floor she wanted, jabbing at it with quite unnecessary violence.

The clang of the lift gates jolted her into the realisation that although the stranger had availed himself of her own name, and had skilfully extracted from her more information about herself than she had been willing to give, he had volunteered no clue as to his own identity.

All that she had to remember him by was a pair of cool grey eyes, and a set of dolphin-engraved cuff-links. And the knowledge that he used one of London's premier hotels as a venue for his appointments.

With whom?

# CHAPTER TWO

THE question continued to tease Kit when she finally made her way home by taxi, this time courtesy of the publishers, who knew about flappy portfolios too.

The solidly built black cab contrasted to its discredit with the luxurious Jaguar car, and, ill at ease now in body as well as in mind, Kit felt weary and cross when she finally paid off the cab driver, added a tip of a size which reflected her relief at being home, and mounted the short flight of stairs to her first-floor flat.

'What a day!'

'Has it been as bad as that?'

Kit spun round, her door half open. 'Hello, Maggie. I didn't realise I'd spoken out loud. It's got me talking to myself now. It's been that kind of a day.'

'I heard the cab. Where's your Metro?'

'By now, wherever good Metros go when they die suddenly, and horribly.'

Unexpectedly, Kit's voice wobbled. The day was still not quite over.

'You haven't had an accident, have you? Are you hurt?'

'Not that sort of an accident, and no, I'm not hurt. Only the Metro.'

'Do you want time to yourself for a quiet howl, or a cup of tea and tell me all about it?'

'A cup of tea. I don't want to howl.'

'You should. You people who keep a stiff upper lip don't do yourself any favours. If I'd had a husband who treated me the way Paul treated you, I'd have cried, screamed, had hysterics and thrown things, and got it out of my system.'

'Work served the same purpose, for me.'

'*Work*!' Maggie snorted, and Kit digressed hastily,

'Come in. I'll put the kettle on, and we can talk in comfort.'

'I'm in my curlers.'

'That means a date. Is he new?'

The latest instalment of Maggie's love-life would provide a bit of light relief, and perhaps ease the tension from her so that she would be able to sleep, Kit hoped.

'What's he like?' she drew her neighbour on.

'New, and *very* nice,' Maggie grinned. 'The date isn't until tomorrow. The curlers are just preliminary groundwork.'

'That doesn't tell me what he's like.'

'This one is the strong, reliable type. Trustworthy.'

'All men are trustworthy, until they're found out.'

Bitter memories ironed out the wobble, and hardened Kit's voice, which rose in indignation when she entered the tiny hallway of the flat, and picked up a pile of letters from the mat.

'Why don't these people take notice when you tell them something?' she cried her exasperation, and held out a couple of brown manila envelopes for Maggie to see. 'They're both bills, and they're both still addressed to Mrs Venables. I've asked them to alter my name at least half a dozen times, and after all these months it still hasn't got through to their records.'

Maggie shrugged philosophically. 'They'll say the computer made the mistake. They always do. That machine is the best scapegoat the human race has had, since Adam put the blame on Eve.'

'Just like a man.' Kit tossed the bills on to the table, and turned into the kitchenette to put the kettle on. Maggie followed her, opining cheerfully,

'Men are rotten, I know, but we can't do without them.'

'I can, from now on.'

'You'll find yourself someone else, one day.'

'I don't intend to go looking.'

The conviction in Kit's voice brought a frown to her friend's forehead. 'You'll have to learn to let go some time, Kit. You'll never find any peace until you do.'

'Paul let go of me, before I even knew...' Kit concentrated hard on filling up the kettle, glad of the excuse to turn her back on her friend for a moment.

Behind her, Maggie declared forcefully, 'If it had been me, I should have known that something was wrong. You're too trusting by half. But I suppose I was brought up more street-wise than you were. I mean, having a couple of archaeologists for parents...' Her cheerful grin returned, taking the sting out of her words.

Kit about-faced, her poise restored by Maggie's sheer normality. 'I suppose our home life, such as it was in between Mother and Dad disappearing on one dig or another, was a bit other-worldly.' She smiled slightly, remembering, and, encouraged by the smile, Maggie hurried on,

'You mean they've always got their heads buried in something or other BC, and they haven't caught on to the fact that the rest of the world is living in the twentieth century.

They're poppets, both of them,' she consoled, 'but all three of you were innocents abroad when it came to someone like your late, un-lamented spouse. You ought to learn to be more like me. No regrets. Love, and let go.'

'You're hopeless, Maggie.' Kit's smile widened as she poured out, and handed a cup of steaming brew across the table to her friend. 'But you've never actually committed yourself. It isn't so easy to let go, once you've been married.'

There was so much shared. So many exper-iences. So much of one another . . .

Maggie sipped thoughtfully, grimaced, and helped herself generously to sugar. 'I'll know, right enough, when the man I want to marry comes along. He'll have something the others haven't got.'

'You'll have plenty of ex-boyfriends to compare him with,' Kit teased. 'You're an out-rageous flirt.'

'That was part of your trouble. You only ever had Paul.'

Kit used her own cup of tea to save herself from having to reply. Paul had been enough. Paul had been her world, ever since their college days together. How did you piece together a broken world?

She replaced her cup on to its saucer, carefully, fitting it exactly into the small inner circle, and said in a voice that was commendably level, 'You're wrong, Maggie. I have let Paul go.'

'But not the hurt he caused you. You've lost all confidence in yourself.'

'I'm working on it.' Kit switched subjects adroitly. 'Tell me about your latest boyfriend. What does he look like?'

'You'll see him on Saturday. He's calling for me here, and we're going to stay with his people for the weekend.'

'Mmm, it sounds serious. But I shan't be here on Saturday.' Kit remembered the subject of her talk with her publisher. 'I've got another assignment. Abroad, this time.'

'You're the jammy one! A fortnight in the Weald of Kent, and now where?'

'The Caribbean. They want me to illustrate Alton Manning's latest book. It's set among the islands there.'

'Phew!' Maggie's whistle was awed. 'You've really hit the big time, doing Alton Manning's work. His books are flavour of the month.'

'I know. I was thrilled when they told me. It's quite a feather in my cap.'

'He ought to be pleased, as well, to get an illustrator like you,' Maggie said loyally. 'I wish

I was coming with you,' she added wistfully. 'I'd give a lot to be let loose on the Caribbean islands for—how long did you say?'

'I didn't. But I should be away for between six to eight weeks, depending on the kind of sketching which the book demands.'

'Have you read it?'

'Not yet. I've got a copy of the manuscript in my portfolio, to take with me. And don't imagine it will be a holiday. I'm not exactly being let loose, as you call it. I'm to stay with some friends of Alton Manning's, at their house on one of the islands, and his nephew has apparently agreed to take me round the others so that I can soak in the atmosphere of the ones he mentions in his book, before I start sketching. I'm going there to work, not to play,' she added severely.

Maggie wrinkled her nose. 'That's another thing, with you. You've forgotten how to play, since Paul. Remember what they say about all work and no play?'

'My name isn't Jack.'

Wisely Maggie left it at that, and shortly afterwards she made her exit, but as Kit drifted off to sleep later her friend's words returned to plague her mind.

'You've forgotten how to play...'

The tiny, engraved figure of a leaping dolphin superimposed itself on Maggie's homily. Dolphins were playful creatures. Friendly and playful. Maybe she would see some, in the sunny waters of the Caribbean.

Kit felt a tremendous sense of a burden being lifted when her plane took off. In the UK there were too many memories. Being in another county was no escape. She had been in most of them already, with Paul. The width of an ocean would surely help her to put her life into perspective again. She watched the coastline of her homeland disappear into the distance, with a sigh of relief.

Perhaps this was what Maggie meant by letting go. Kit supposed she should have done it before, but there had been no opportunity for her to get right away. There had been so many things to claim her attention in the winding up of Paul's affairs, bona fide and otherwise, and then afterwards there were the paintings needed for the countryside calender.

Deliberately, she had buried herself in her work. Searching for suitable subjects had kept her constantly on the move, capturing the most picturesque scenery in more than a dozen counties, one for each month of the year, working assiduously on several pictures in each county so that the publishers had a wide final choice.

The last county, Kent, had led to the demise of her Metro.

But that, too, was behind her now, for the next several weeks at least. Kit relaxed in her seat, and searched out the as yet unread manuscript from her cabin baggage.

It was a testimony to the power of the author's pen that the stewardess had to speak to her twice before she roused from her absorption, to the realisation that a lot of miles had passed unnoticed beneath her, and a meal was being served. She ate abstractedly, begrudging the time spent away from the manuscript.

Alton Manning brought the Caribbean islands to life. In a fast-moving tale of crime and passion, his characters visited nearly every one. Kit studied the map which accompanied the manuscript. Antigua, Grenada, St Lucia...the names held all the fascination of sunny skies, and cobalt seas.

Translated, they also meant a good deal of art work to be done, and she began to appreciate the reason for her publisher's relaxed time-table—he had told her, 'You'll be gone for about six to eight weeks at least.'

'Surely I shan't need so long?'

'You may need even longer. If you do, take it. Manning can well afford to pay. Indeed, I know he's prepared to, in order to get the kind of pictures he wants to illustrate his book. He's a perfectionist.'

Kit hoped that Alton Manning's nephew was aware of that, too, since he was destined to be her escort round the islands. She wondered idly if he had volunteered, or had had to have his arm twisted before he had agreed to give up his time to be her guide.

She forked dutifully at her meal, and tried to imagine what it was the unknown nephew did for a living that would enable him to have time off to take her round. She hoped it would be sufficient for her to be able to thoroughly absorb the atmosphere of the places she saw. That was as essential as the actual art work, and was something that could not be hurried, since the one without the other was lifeless.

'Take all the time you need. A break will do you good,' her publisher had told her kindly, and on her return to the flat Maggie had echoed his well-meaning advice with,

'Take time off to play, while you're out there. Don't spend every single second working. Live dangerously. Take a swimsuit with you.'

'I don't suppose I shall have time.'

'Make time. Take one anyway. It will tuck into a corner of your suitcase.'

Kit had packed the swimsuit, and suddenly she felt glad that she had given in to Maggie. Warm blue seas did sound inviting, and it was a long time since she had gone swimming. It had been her favourite sport before she got married. She had abandoned it then. Paul had had no time for sports of any kind. He preferred partying.

I'll take it up again after I get back, Kit promised herself, and smiled inwardly. Maggie had been right, as usual. Even at this distance, the islands of the Caribbean were beginning to work their magic spell.

It was pouring with rain when she landed.

Kit surveyed the leaden skies with a distinct feeling of let-down. Nothing she had read about the Caribbean had prepared her for this. A shiver ran through her. It was not cold, just damply clammy. The shiver was mostly psychological, a hangover from the dark cloud of depression that was always in the background these days, waiting to pounce.

There was nothing even remotely cold in the manner of the woman who hurried to greet her when Kit emerged from Customs.

'Anyone toting that kind of portfolio simply *has* to be Kit Fielding.' Her smile was as warm as her flawless honey-coloured complexion. 'We've been so looking forward to meeting you,' she cried. 'When Alton let us know you were coming out here to illustrate his new book, we insisted upon your staying with us.'

Kit thought, Alton Manning extends his policy of perfection to his friends, as well as to his work. The woman hurrying towards her was extraordinarily beautiful. Queenly. Kit felt a flash of envy at the other's model height, which she carried with a natural grace. She was like a lovely painting come to life, and Kit's hands urged to reach for her paintbrushes and canvas. Instead, she found them taken in an eager clasp.

'I'm Lois. My husband, here, is Jesse. May we call you Kit?'

Friendly hands folded her own. Warm smiles embraced her. This, and not the weather, was the real spirit of the Caribbean, Kit decided. She felt an unexpected lump rise in her throat, and had to swallow quickly before she could manage, with a return smile, 'Oh, yes, please do.'

'Take no notice of the weather,' Lois implored her. 'The rain here never lasts for long. As soon as the sun comes out, it will dry us off.'

Her unprotected hair, as black as her sparkling eyes, shone with raindrops, as did that of her husband, Kit noticed. Jesse met her glance with an infectious grin which made a white gleam in his attractive dark face.

'We'll all start to steam any minute now.'

As if at a signal, an answering gleam, hot and golden, thrust through parting clouds, redeeming the reputation of the islands, and Kit's spirits rose to match as Jesse took charge of her luggage and stowed it in the back of a pick-up before telling her briskly, 'The anchorage isn't far from here. After that, there's only a short sea trip, and we'll soon be home,' generously inviting his guest to regard his home as her own for the duration of her stay. Seeing her enquiring look, he enlarged, 'Home is further along the coast from here. We're on the leeward side of the island, so it's nice for bathing.'

He set the pick-up rolling, and Kit's foot tapped irrepressibly in time to the insistent beat of reggae which reached her from half a dozen radio sets parked among the colourful stalls of fruit lining the roadway, all steaming gently in the strengthening sun, as Jesse had predicted.

'I hope you've brought a costume with you?' Lois said, and Kit sent up a silent Thank-you to Maggie as she answered,

'Yes, I put one in my luggage, although it's some time since I used it.'

Too long. And by her present measurements the costume would probably be too big. She had been silly to shut the door on her favourite pastime, merely to please Paul, she realised too late. Lois opened it again for her with, 'Jesse and I swim every day. You must join us. You'll love it. The sea is always calm and warm on our side of the island. Ideal for a dip.'

'I thought it was always like that, all over the Caribbean? The holiday brochures...'

'Only tell you the best bits,' Lois laughed. 'On the Atlantic side of the islands, the sea can be quite rough, and there's a strong wind. It isn't really a good idea to swim there. There are a lot of currents and undertows, and often the sea bed is quite rocky. The sloping sandy beaches on the leeward side are much nicer.'

Two faces to the islands. One, gentle and be-guiling. The other, treacherous and rough, with hidden dangers waiting to pounce on the unwary. Just like life, Kit thought bleakly, and, watching her, Lois misinterpreted her guest's suddenly sober look, and hastened to reassure her.

'Don't worry, the currents aren't strong enough to put the boat in any danger. Jesse knows every inch of the sea all round the islands. He uses the boat daily for his work, to travel between them.'

'See for yourself what a sturdy little craft she is,' Jesse invited as he braked the pick-up to a halt and led the way along a landing-stage to where a small but efficient-looking cutter bobbed up and down at the end of a line of moored craft.

'It's a nice way to travel,' Kit remarked appreciatively as he helped her on board.

'Most of the islands have got decent roads by now,' Jesse admitted. 'After the last bad hurricane there was a massive rebuilding programme, and the roads were improved along with the buildings. But having my own boat means that I don't have to wait for the islander. That's the local inter-island plane service,' he explained. 'With my own transport, I'm not restricted as to the luggage I can carry, either. That's a help because I often need to take along equipment, or bring back specimens.'

'Jesse is an agricultural scientist,' Lois explained as she settled herself in the small open cabin beside Kit, while her husband took the wheel of the little craft and sent it skimming across the surface of the bay towards the open sea.

'Engaged on what?' Kit asked interestedly.

'Research into animal and plant diseases.'

'That isn't quite so horrendous as it sounds,' Jesse threw over his shoulder, while keeping his eyes alert to guide them through the miscellany of leisure and working craft moored in the bay.

'We've succeeded in eradicating a lot of the old problems which used to plague the growers out here,' he went on. 'The coconut palms on some of the islands are a case in point. The new ones are not so tall. They may not please the romantics, but shorter trees are an advantage in such a hurricane-prone area, and they've got an in-built resistance to a lot of the bugs which used to afflict the older varieties. It will take time to prove their worth, of course.'

'You must need lots of patience. It will take ages before you see any results,' Kit responded, and Jesse nodded.

'Decades, sometimes,' he agreed cheerfully, and raised his hand to answer a wave from another boat. 'It needs long-term commitment, if you want to see the results of any kind of research.'

Long-term commitment was the one attribute which Paul had lacked. He had been a 'today' person, for whom *now* was everything. Kit's gaze brooded on the water, her artist's eye automatically registering the incredible range of liquid colour, from deepest blue to clear emerald-green.

Fleur Joyner-Galloway's eyes were green. Cat's eyes, cold, calculating and cruel, totally devoid of tears for the loss of the man whom she had stolen from another woman, to be her lover.

Kit had only seen her rival once, when they had both appeared at the coroner's inquest. Not even Fleur had had the audacity to attend Paul's funeral. Kit doubted if she would have wanted to anyway. Fleur was a 'now' person, too. Regret of any kind was not her scene.

'Welcome home.' Jesse broke across Kit's reverie with a wide sweep of his arm, which encompassed a scene that took her breath away. He throttled the engine down to a quiet stutter, and allowed his craft to coast gently into the most perfect natural harbour that Kit had ever seen.

Distant peaks rose, sharp-edged against the sky. Green forest tumbled down steep hillsides, to fringe a beach of creamy sand, which looked as if no human foot had trodden its surface since the world began. Twin arms of rock guarded the narrow entrance to the bay, which widened into a circular harbour of almost perfect dimensions.

Jesse remarked with satisfaction, 'This is one of the safest anchorages on the island. When a hurricane is blowing, it's full of craft seeking shelter.'

there was only one boat riding its waters at the moment, a large, sea-going yacht, of a size that looked as if it would easily ride out the worst storm. Eyeing it, Kit thought with awe, there could only be inches to spare between the ship's sides, and the two arms of rock guarding the harbour entrance. Whoever skippered the vessel must have supreme confidence in his own navigational powers, to take it through such a tight channel.

As they drew closer, the name painted on the side of the yacht caught her eye. The *Dolphin*. Dolphins seemed to be following her around just lately, Kit decided wryly, and bent interested eyes on the small tender which was drawn up on the beach, its twinned name proclaiming it as belonging to the yacht.

There *were* footsteps on the sand, after all, she discovered. They led from the tender, up the gently sloping beach towards the trees. Widely spaced footsteps, denoting a long stride, and leading straight away in a purposeful line, as if the strider knew exactly where he was going, and what it was he intended to do when he got there.

Lois remarked, 'We're lucky. Our house is sheltered from the force of the wind, as well as the bay. During the last big blow even the houses that were still left standing mostly had their roofs blown off, but ours stayed intact.'

'It's a good job it did, with the number of people we packed under it, until their own were repaired again,' Jesse remembered ruefully.

Their roof was about to shelter another refugee, this time from a different kind of storm, Kit reflected as she stepped ashore, and tilted her head the better to view her home for the next few weeks.

The house was built into the hillside, on two generous levels, with a wide veranda running the whole length of the upper storey, a perfect situation from which to enjoy a perfect view.

A path led upwards through the trees from the edge of the beach. The footsteps in the sand finished where it began, but although Kit's eyes searched the line of the path which wound in easy stages through a garden brilliant with flowering shrubs she could see no sign of the man who had made them. Judging by the depths of the imprints in the sand, and the length of stride between them, it had to be a man, she judged.

Jesse said, 'I'll bring your case up now, and come back for my equipment later.'

'I'll carry my case,' Kit protested. 'You bring your equipment, and save yourself another journey.'

'It's no hassle,' her host said amiably. 'Brook will help me with the equipment. He's got here before us.'

Brook, presumably, being the man who made the footprints in the sand. Kit strolled beside Lois up the sloping path, her lungs taking in deep, blissful breaths of the perfumed air.

'You live in Paradise!' she exclaimed, and Lois shot her a thoughtful look.

'It can be just the opposite, when the storms blow. But on balance I'd rather endure those than live somewhere else.'

There was always a serpent... But at least the storms Lois spoke of were of the impersonal kind. The wounds they inflicted could only be physical.

'Come and meet Brook,' Lois urged her. 'He's Alton's nephew. The one who's taking you round to see the islands.'

Was he a volunteer, or a pressed man? The still unanswered question sent a prick of unease through Kit. The strong line of footprints had looked uncompromising.

'We practically live out here.' Lois led her up a short flight of steps on to the wide veranda, and Kit walked across to the white-painted rail.

'What a superb view. I can't wait to start sketching.'

'Meet your guide first,' Lois smiled, and turned to the man who came in with Jesse through an inner door.

'Brook, come and meet . . .'

'*Kit Fielding*!'

He was dressed differently. White shorts, socks and deck shoes replaced the classic business suit, and his snowy shirt boasted neither cuff-links nor tie. Instead, it was open at the neck to reveal a length of strong, tanned throat and chest that did uncomfortable things to Kit's metabolism as she stared back at him in dismay.

In spite of the difference in dress, there could be no mistake. It was the same man. Recognition was instant, and mutual.

'*Kit Fielding*!' he exclaimed again.

Kit's eyes widened with a mixture of shock and disbelief, and her tongue recalled the only identity which she had to remember him by.

'The man with the dolphin cuff-links.'

## CHAPTER THREE

'YOU'RE observant, to notice such a small thing as a cuff-link,' he said.

His eyes narrowed, watching her, their expression unreadable behind hooded lids. Kit flushed. He made it sound as if she had been ogling him, that day in the restaurant. She denied any such intention with a terse, 'Artists are trained to be observant. It's their job. The same as policemen.'

She turned to Lois. 'I met—er——'

'Brook,' he insisted, and her colour deepened.

Using his first name shortened the distance between them. The distance which, these days, she kept between herself and all men. But Lois had omitted his surname from the introduction, denying her its use. It would be Manning, of course, the same as his uncle, the author, but the relaxed friendliness of her host and hostess made first names obligatory, and it would seem stiff and stand-offish if she did not go along with them. Kit capitulated unwillingly.

'Brook . . .' She had to force the word out. 'Brook offered me a lift to London, when a van destroyed my Metro. I needed to get some work to my publisher, to meet a printing deadline,' she excused her acceptance of his help, and added offhandedly to Brook, 'I didn't know then, of course, that Alton Manning was your uncle.'

If she had known, and had been aware that the author would press his nephew into service as her guide, would she have accepted the commission? Brook exuded a compelling attraction which found chinks in her armour which she had thought to be impregnable.

She could feel the attraction now, like a magnetic field surrounding him, drawing her. She steeled herself against its pull as Jesse put in, 'It's nice that you two already know one another. There are a lot of islands to get round in the time you're here, Kit. Alton didn't miss out many from his book. He's got a great affection for the Caribbean. It's his second home.'

'Does he have one here? A home, I mean?' Kit drove the conversation on, grasping at irrelevances to keep at bay the dropping silence which would give Brook an opening to breach it, and her own fragile defences.

'Not a home of his own. He usually comes to stay with us, or if Brook has got the *Dolphin* in the area he sometimes stays on the yacht. He calls it his floating island. It gives him peace in which to write uninterrupted.'

Kit nodded. She understood the need. It was exactly the same with painting. She said impulsively, 'I shan't need to see all of the islands. One or two should be sufficient to give me enough local colour.'

That would let her guide off the hook, she reasoned, and it would also limit the amount of time she needed to spend in his company. She dismissed her own vulnerability as a reason, preferring to excuse herself on the grounds that it would reduce her obligation to Brook, which was beginning to rankle even before it had begun.

'That's where you're wrong.' Unexpectedly Brook defended her need to see all of the named islands. 'Each island is different from the next,' he insisted, as she opened her mouth to protest.

'But, surely——'

'Brook's right,' Jesse backed him up. 'Although they're so close to each other, the geography of the islands differs widely, as do the people. They each have their own unique culture and lifestyle, and they defend it vigorously. They're very proud of their own heritage. They don't even trade much, one with another. Mostly the produce from the islands is exported abroad, a lot of it to Europe, which is where Brook comes in.'

Brook? Kit's questioning glance in the direction of her guide-to-be asked a question, and Jesse answered it with, 'He's head of the Dolphin Line. Didn't you know?'

Kit shook her head. They had not got that far, during their car ride to London. Only as far as Brook learning all he wanted to know about her, but not giving away any information about himself. What she had just learned made her rescuer's casual mention of an appointment at Claridge's seem as normal as 'let's meet under the station clock'.

'You must have heard of the Dolphin Line?' Jesse urged, and Kit mumbled,

'Yes, of course I've heard of them.'

Who had not heard of the vast merchant shipping fleet, whose activities spanned the globe? And this man was its head.

It explained the beautifully engraved cuff-links, the name on the yacht and its tender, and the suddenly hollow feeling in the pit of Kit's stomach, as she absorbed the fact that the head of this immense world-wide enterprise had been pressed into service to act in the capacity of what amounted to little more than a tourist guide.

Happily unaware of her dismay, Jesse went on, 'It's the difference between them which makes the islands so fascinating.'

'It's also the reason I tried to persuade Alton to engage a local artist to illustrate his book,' Brook put in evenly. 'There's plenty of good talent on the islands themselves, but he wouldn't listen.'

Good for Alton Manning! Kit applauded silently. It would take a brave determination to resist Brook. But the latter's opposition to his relative made her own position here even less tenable, she realised unhappily.

A local artist would not have needed a guide, which confirmed that Brook had probably been pressed into service, just as she had feared, and his reluctance was obvious, and understandable now she knew his circumstances.

Her spirits sank. It did not augur well for the time they would be obliged to spend in one another's company.

'I can understand Alton's reason for engaging an artist from the outside,' Lois put in thoughtfully, and Brook drawled,

'Tell me.'

He leaned back in a relaxed attitude against the white-painted veranda rail, and stretched

tanned arms along its wooden top, a lithe, athletic figure whose dark head and clean-cut
profile made a perfect contrast to the colourful
backdrop of lagoon, and yacht, and . . .

With an effort, Kit dragged her mind away
from art, and concentrated on argument.

'Tell me,' Brook had invited, and the look
on his face had said that the reason would have
to be a good one to convince him.

'It's logical, if you think about it,' Lois
answered, in no way put off. 'The vast ma-
jority of Alton's readers will never have been
to the Caribbean, and aren't likely to. So he
would want his book jacket, and the illustrations which go with the text, to be the kind of
things that would most strike a newcomer to
the islands.'

'Like the woman at the fruit stall, on the way
from the airport!' Kit exclaimed. 'She was
plaiting her little girl's hair while she waited
for customers. The child had got a gap between her two front teeth when she smiled.'

Loving children, Kit had waved, and the
small girl had waved back and smiled, revealing the gap.

'Those things would strike a local artist, too,'
Brook argued, and Lois nodded.

'Of course they would. But to a local they
would be everyday, familiar things, and un-

important because of that. A local would most likely go for the big and the spectacular, illustrating the common perception of the Caribbean. Beaches, palm trees, forests . . . things like that.'

'Promoting the tourist Caribbean,' Brook said drily.

'Exactly, whereas fresh eyes, particularly a woman's eyes—— ' Lois's smile at Kit made a small, warm link between them '—a woman's eyes will look for something they can relate to. Smaller, more intimate things. A bird in the forest, rather than the forest itself. The little girl with the gap in her teeth.'

Kit returned Lois's smile, and thought, She's a shrewd psychologist, as well as a teacher. Perhaps the two went together.

'Kit notices people,' Lois went on, and Brook drawled,

'So I've discovered.'

He gave no quarter, Kit thought uneasily, and her hand strayed upwards to tuck her hair behind her ear in the old, nervous gesture, but Lois was not tuned in to undercurrents, and continued happily, 'So she's ideal for the job. Alton's book is all about people.'

Brook was people, too, and he would certainly never go unnoticed, in whatever company he happened to be, but . . . relate to him? Kit swallowed on a suddenly dry throat. In the weeks that followed, she was going to have to learn to do just that.

The swallow helped. It allowed her voice to come through cool and contained. 'I could make other arrangements to be taken round the islands.' She had no idea how, or with whom, but it stated her independence, and she continued more confidently, 'I don't want to put you to any inconvenience. You needn't feel under any obligation to act as my guide.'

The obligation she was already under to Brook still rankled. There was still the matter of the restaurant bill. She would watch for an opportunity, and make sure she paid him back for that while she was here, she determined.

'I gave my word to Alton,' he answered her flatly, in a tone that allowed no argument. Evidently he regarded his word as his bond, as well as law. Kit chalked up a reluctant point in his favour as he continued, 'In any case, I've got business round the islands, so you might as well tag along. Consider yourself as deck cargo,' he grinned, and Kit's lips tightened.

Deck cargo, indeed!

Brook's smile widened, seeing his shaft reach its target. 'If you come along with me, you'll see people and places tourists never reach. It will be all the better for Alton's book.'

'Have you read it?' Kit asked guardedly, and he answered,

'Of course.'

No doubt he also had his own ideas as to how the book should be illustrated. If he had, he could keep them to himself, Kit decided hardily. Where her work was concerned, it was her ideas which counted, and not his.

She wished she could ignore his smile. She shifted uneasily in her seat. It was disarming. Dangerous. In it lurked the mischievous smile of a schoolboy. It warmed the grey of his eyes, and softened the stern line of his jaw, and heightened by several disconcerting notches the sheer male magnetism of the man, which, if she was not careful, he might use to undermine her resistance if it came to a clash of wills between them. She would not put such a ploy past him.

When Brook called for Kit the next morning, his smile was still in evidence, but it was no longer that of a mischievous schoolboy, but the smile of a man, and it held a hint of triumph.

Kit sat sketching on the beach. Jesse had set off in the cutter for one of the other islands, and Lois was engaged with her pupils, but, although Kit dutifully laid out her sketching materials, her pencil idled on her pad, and her mind refused to settle to her work.

It felt all wrong to be sitting alone on a palm-fringed beach. Pale sand and blue water made a dazzling contrast to beguile an artist's eye, and the sun spilled her shadow in a stubby finger in front of her.

A solitary shadow. It was like sitting at a table for one.

Kit felt restless, and tense. When Brook had left after dinner the previous evening, he'd told her, 'I'll come back for you, in the morning.'

He did not specify at what time, and Kit determined that, when he did arrive, he would not find her meekly waiting for him. He would discover her already fully occupied, and independent of his services if he did not feel like giving them.

The reality was like waiting at the dentist's, she decided ruefully. Except that this waiting was much worse. The discomfort at the dentist's only lasted for a short time, whereas the strain of being in Brook's company could go on for weeks.

Impatiently Kit shrugged away the thought of Brook, and bent her head with renewed determination over her pad, and such was the self-discipline which she had learned during the past year that she eventually became absorbed in her sketching, so that when the yacht arrived it slid unnoticed through the harbour entrance.

Brook did not bring his vessel right into the lagoon, as he had done the previous day. He anchored it just inside the twin arms of rock, and came ashore in the tender, but the light breeze which rustled the palm leaves above Kit's head muffled the sound of his oars, and he added his shadow to her own before she realised with a start that she was no longer alone.

Her hair had flopped over one eye, getting in the way of her clear vision, and automatically she raised her hand to tuck it back again behind her ear.

Other hands forestalled her. Lean brown fingers, which had fixed the lock of her seatbelt the week before, reached down and lifted the lock of hair away from her eyes, and smoothed down the silky curtain as their owner's voice asked, 'Have you lost your grip?'

She was losing her grip fast, but not in the way Brook meant. The touch of his hand on her hair made her whole scalp tingle as if with an electric shock, and Kit jerked into a vivid awareness of him standing behind her.

Her fingers closed over the 2B pencil she was using, with a convulsive grip which threatened to snap the fragile lead, but the wood was tougher, and withstood the sudden pressure, hurting her with a sharp pain which jolted her jangled nerves back into sufficient control to enable her to stammer, 'I—I don't use grips. They won't stay fixed.'

The soft brown curtain stubbornly resisted the grasp of anything which Kit put in to try to confine it, but in Brook's hands it lingered, as if loving the feel of his fingers that raked through its shining length, drawing it back from her face ... Drawing her face up, and back, tilting it to meet Brook's lips as he pressed them firmly down to cover her own.

Kit was trembling all over when he released her. Her eyes, wide and shocked, stared up into his, and met in his smile the triumph of conquest. She blinked rapidly to loosen the spell, and an involuntary gasp broke from her lips.

'Did I startle you?'

He knew that he had, and he was enjoying her fright. Kit got out, 'I ... you ...'

Maggie had urged her to, 'Take time off, to play.'

She did not want to play at this game, Kit thought raggedly. Not ever again. And least of all with Brook.

He remarked, as if nothing out of the ordinary had happened between them, 'If you're ready, shall we go?'

Kit drew in a hard breath. 'I've got everything I need with me.' She strove to match Brook's casual tone, but, in spite of her best efforts, the words came out jerky and uncertain, and she bent swiftly to gather up her pencils and snap them into their box, using the move to hide her glowing face, while she strove unavailingly to rescue her poise.

The box safely closed, she slid it along with her sketch-block into her portfolio, and pulled the zip shut. It was a much smaller portfolio she was using this time, which was easier for her to carry.

'You haven't got your swimsuit,' Brook discovered, his sharp eyes registering the lack.

Kit straightened, her equipment in her hand. 'I shan't need a swimsuit, only when I'm back here with Lois and Jesse.'

Her look in Brook's direction was wary. Was he trying to trap her into wasting time, so that he could report back to his uncle, and have her recalled? He had made no secret of his preference for a local artist to illustrate Alton Manning's book, and Lois's argument the night before had signally failed to convince him. Suspicion sharpened Kit's voice as she added firmly, 'I'm coming along with you to work, not to go swimming.' Let Brook play alone, if he wanted to.

He gave her a quizzical look. 'You can't paint warm blue seas unless you've swum in them, and felt their warmth for yourself. If you do, your paintings will be lifeless, and unconvincing.'

Kit bit her lip. Brook was so right. And he knew it, she thought tartly. His rightness rankled. She would have liked to denounce it, but she was here to soak up atmosphere, whether literally or otherwise, and the temptation to repeat the delicious pleasure of her early morning swim with Lois and Jesse tipped the scales of her reluctance.

'I'll go and fetch it, then, just in case I've got the time.' She emphasised her right to decide for herself when the time came whether she would use it or not, and despised her feet for the haste with which they hurried her up the path to collect the amber-coloured one-piece from where it hung across the veranda rail, already dried in the hot sunshine from its use some hours earlier. She stuffed it into its waterproof bag along with the towel, and was surprised at the sudden lifting of her spirits as she hurried back to rejoin Brook on the beach.

He had her small portfolio in his hand. He seemed to have developed a habit of annexing her portfolios, Kit thought vexedly, and held out her hand for it with a determined, 'I'll carry it.'

'I'll carry you both.' Before she realised what Brook was about to do, he scooped her high in his arms with a calm, 'It would be a pity to get your sandals wet.'

Brook himself had waded ashore barefoot, leaving the tender bobbing in knee-deep water some distance from the shore. His knee-deep would almost sink her, Kit realised with dismay, but she would rather get wet than endure the indignity of being carried. She attempted to struggle out of his arms.

'Put me down. I'm quite capable of wading out myself.'

His darkly tanned shoulder, inadequately covered by his open-down-the-front shirt, made tingling contact with her bare cheek, and Kit jerked her face away from its touch, and risked a crick in her neck as she held her head stiffly unsupported. Brook stopped, and looked down into her face while they were still long feet of deep water away from the tender.

'If you don't lie still,' he told her mildly, 'I'll drop you in the bay.'

'You wouldn't dare.'

'Try me.'

She was not prepared to. Her angry eyes measured his look, but caution warned her that if the worst happened her portfolio might well follow her into the water. It was reasonably waterproof against the British weather, but it was not guaranteed to protect its contents against being dunked in the Caribbean sea, and she was not prepared to risk ruining her precious sketch-block and pencils. Her lashes dropped, shielding her from the glint in the grey pools above her, which posed the question, Would he kiss her again?

His lips refrained, but the laugh in his eyes was another kind of caress, and Kit lay stiffly still in his arms, hating its echo that lifted the corners of his well-cut lips.

He recommenced wading, and seconds later placed her neatly in the tender, put her portfolio down beside her on the hard wooden seat, and added the impertinent instruction, 'Don't drop it overboard.'

She would dearly love to hurl it at his arrogant head, Kit fumed silently, and had to grab at the seat as Brook vaulted into the tender, and nearly rocked her off balance.

She tore her eyes away from the sight of strong, flowing muscles which became a smooth extension of the expertly wielded oars as Brook pulled away from the beach towards the yacht, and she let out an inaudible sigh of relief when they finally gained its deck, and he tied the tender securely to the rail with the remark, 'Two minutes, and we'll be under way.'

For a while at least he would be busy navigating the vessel, which would give her time to regain her poise. To help her recovery along, Kit asked, 'Aren't you going to use the sails?'

The yacht was a nice, safe subject to talk about, and it did look oddly naked without its sails, a watered-down version of the dignified vessel which had cruised out of the harbour the evening before. From the safe privacy of her room, Kit had watched it go, excusing herself on the grounds that it was not Brook she was watching, but the dramatic picture his boat made on the lagoon, with a view to sketching it later for his uncle's book.

'Another time,' he answered. 'I use the sails for pleasure, but I use diesel power for working journeys. It's quicker, and more convenient.'

Engrossed in her own problems, Kit had forgotten for the moment that this was a working journey for Brook also. Reminded, she looked round her for the portfolio which he had carried on board, leaving her to climb the ladder to the deck with her swimsuit bag slung over her shoulder, and her hands unimpeded to help her up.

'Where did you put it?' she wanted to know. 'I'll finish off my sketch until we get to wherever we're going.'

'We're heading for the next island but one this morning. I'm going to see a man about some coconuts.'

Kit's swift upwards look accused, Sarcastic! and, although she remained silent, Brook's all-seeing eyes registered her thoughts as accurately as if she had spoken out loud, and he answered her with, 'True. You'll see when we get there. The trip isn't a very long one, so you won't need your sketch-book.'

He did not tell her where he had put her portfolio, and quick indignation rose in Kit. He had no right to withhold her equipment, dictating what she should and should not do, as if she were a child. She burst out, 'I'll decide for myself when I want to sketch.'

Brook turned then, and regarded her for a long moment before he drawled, 'Sheath your claws, kitten.'

'Don't call me kitten,' Kit gritted. She hated this byplay on her name. Paul had used it. At first, when they were courting, she had endured it, telling herself that it was his way of showing affection. Afterwards, she had learned to hate it, when he had used it to torment her, knowing how she felt about it.

'No, ma'am,' Brook mocked, and left Kit unsure whether he was refusing to locate her portfolio for her, or agreeing not to call her kitten. The former, she suspected angrily, but before she could speak again he resumed, 'Lie back and relax. Soak up sensations. Let the islands get under your skin. Your paintings will be all the better for it.'

It was her need to forget sensations of a very different kind which made Kit need her sketching materials so desperately, and it was not the islands, but Brook himself, which threatened to get under her skin. The latter was not thick enough to defend itself against his penetrating charisma, she acknowledged ruefully.

As for relaxing, that was impossible anywhere within Brook's orbit. Nevertheless, Kit stretched out on a deck lounger, feigning indifference, but in spite of the chair's luxurious comfort her nerves remained as tight as a fiddle-string tuned to concert pitch.

She yearned for her sketch-book as never before, for her own sake, as a shield, not simply to work on illustrations for the book, but if she insisted upon having her portfolio Brook might question her burst of enthusiasm, and how could she explain that her need was to fix her eyes on her work in order to prevent them from fixing instead on the sight of broad shoulders swelling beneath a freshly laundered shirt, and a neat dark head showing above the rim of the cockpit, filling her vision to the exclusion of the magnificent scenery sliding by on the other side of the yacht's rail?

The journey went on for long enough to allow the gentle motion of the boat to ease Kit's tension, and insensibly she had begun to relax a little by the time their destination came into view, and Brook brought the yacht round and aimed it towards a long landing-stage which ran far enough out into deep water for the vessel to berth comfortably.

A pick-up truck and a driver met them on the jetty. 'Guessed you were heading our way,' he greeted Brook laconically.

'Hadn't you told them you were coming?' Kit asked, surprised, and Brook smiled.

'You don't need to make appointments in the Caribbean. The islands are so small, everyone knows what everyone else is doing, almost before they know it themselves.'

Kit absorbed this information with the odd feeling that the world was turning upside-down. The transition from brisk, efficient businessman, with an appointment at Claridge's, which she had no doubt Brook had kept on the dot, to the casual, easygoing creature who, she noticed, was not even wearing his watch, and left the local grapevine to make his appointments for him, was startling.

She glanced up into his face, to find he was watching her, reading her thoughts from the expression on her own. To mask them, Kit tossed out a flippant, 'Laid-back, eh?'

'Almost horizontal,' Brook agreed gravely, with a quirky lift to his eyebrows that sent the blood rushing to Kit's cheeks.

There was nothing in the least laid-back in the business operation to which the driver took them. Their route led them through thriving groves of coconuts, and Kit avoided Brook's slanting glance in her direction which mocked, I told you so, and concentrated hard on the scene of purposeful activity which met her eyes as their vehicle drew to a halt beside a series of shed-like buildings, from which issued a buzz of activity.

'This is where coconut fibre is turned into garden humus,' Brook explained. 'It's the coming thing in the gardening world, as an alternative to peat. It's stood up very well so far, in experimentation, and it should become widely used among the gardening fraternity. The peat bogs are rapidly becoming exhausted with over-use, and this fibre should help to save those that are left.'

She was learning fast, Kit decided. She had not suspected Brook of being environmentally minded. She scored another cautious point in his favour, and asked curiously, 'Where do you fit into all this?'

'The fibre is exported, and the Dolphin Line has the shipping contract. I'm here to arrange a large shipment to the UK. There's a growing demand for it in the garden centres back home.'

He unlatched the briefcase which he had carried with him from the yacht, and which made an incongruous addition to his casual attire, and withdrew Kit's portfolio.

So that was where he had hidden it! No wonder she had been unable to find it. Kit held out her hand for her possession, in exasperated silence.

'Have a look round,' Brook invited, releasing it to her. 'I've got to go and talk tonnage to the man in charge. You'd find that boring. Go on, everyone is friendly here,' he added as she hesitated. 'No one will mind in the least if you sit and watch them at work, or even sketch them, so long as you ask their permission first.'

He disappeared up the steps of a prefabricated office without waiting for her to reply, and for a moment Kit stood still, undecided what to do. She did not want Brook's company, but she felt oddly bereft without it, until a voice hailed her from a nearby doorway.

'This way, man, if you want to come and see.'

Kit looked round, but by now Brook had disappeared, and there did not seem to be any other man immediately visible. The voice must mean herself. Clutching her portfolio nervously, she stepped through the doorway, and came to a halt as the contrast between bright sunlight and the comparative dusk of the shed left her momentarily unable to focus properly.

As her eyes adjusted to the dimmer light, she became aware of a pair of cut-down shorts, filled by a youth of magnificent physique. She tilted her head back to look up into his face, and met a disarming smile.

Everyone seemed to smile, on the islands. It was the smile which she needed to put into her paintings, to bring them to life, and which had been missing from her work for too long.

'I'm Al,' the youth introduced himself amiably. 'You want to see round? Or have you come to talk freight? If so, you'll need the office.' His smile broadened appreciatively. 'We don't usually have a girl come. As a rule, Brook deals with the business side himself.'

'Brook's in the office now, doing just that.' It was easy to talk to Al, Kit found. Why was it not so easy to talk to Brook? She explained, 'He's brought me along for the ride. I'm illustrating a book with a background based on the islands, and I need to soak in atmosphere.'

'An artist, eh?' Al's interest quickened. 'You must meet Jo. He does paintings. Come and see.'

He led the way to an even dimmer corner of the shed which housed a man busy with a tally board. Behind him, the wooden wall was literally covered with some of the most finely executed seascapes Kit had ever seen, haphazardly drawing-pinned to the planks.

Her eyes widened, and she stepped forward eagerly to examine them. 'Are these all your work?' The man with the tally board nodded, and Kit exclaimed, 'It's sheer vandalism to treat them like this! Work of this calibre deserves to be framed, and exhibited properly.'

Jo grinned, not unpleased with the admiration. 'I do exhibit, now and again, when I get time off from my job here.'

'What a waste! You ought to paint full time.'

'I gotta eat, man.'

The dilemma of artists the world over. Kit nodded sympathetically, and Jo asked her, 'What sort of work are you here to do? Not another tourist brochure?'

'No, I'm illustrating a book. One of Alton Manning's.'

'I know his writing,' her fellow artist answered interestedly. 'He's real good. When does the book come out?'

'Quite soon now. It's only waiting for the illustrations, for printing to begin.'

'I'll look out for it. I'll be interested to see your work, too,' he said, and added generously, 'If you like, I can show you places where you can get seascapes like these.'

'Maybe for the book jacket,' Kit said doubtfully, 'but for the text I need something smaller, more intimate. Something which the reader can easily relate to.'

'Such as?'

Kit told him about the child with the gap in her teeth. 'Things like that. Little, typical things about life on the islands.'

'People things,' Jo said instantly, latching on to Kit's wavelength with ease. 'Try walking uphill along that track through the trees.' He pointed through another wide-open door at the other end of the shed. 'You might find some ideas there. Not people. The village is further on. But there's a lot of wild bushes in flower, and butterflies and birds. They'd come under much the same heading, I reckon.'

He understood! Warmed by her contact with a fellow artist, Kit smiled her thanks, and followed his direction, and she found the flowers, and forgot the butterflies, in the fascination of watching humming-birds feeding from the brilliant blooms, tiny darting specks of brilliant colour, which defied the eye with the swiftness of their flight.

Entranced, she settled in the shade of a nearby tree to sketch, and lost count of time until Brook remarked from just behind her, 'Very pretty. But it will be of no use for Alton's book. As far as I can remember, he didn't mention humming-birds in any of the chapters.'

Brook was interfering, just as Kit had feared he might. If she allowed it to pass, it would happen again, and again, and the work which she eventually presented to her publisher would be more Brook's ideas than her own. It was now or never, to make a stand against him. Striving to control her temper, Kit said stiffly, 'Nor so far as I can remember, either.'

'Then why bother to sketch humming-birds?'

'My instructions, *from your uncle*,' Kit shot back through set teeth, 'are to do a series of sketches and paintings which relate directly to the scenes in his book, and then some more which are simply typical of the islands.

Humming-birds feeding off flowers are obviously typical of this particular island.'

'And . . . ?'

'And I intend to follow my usual policy of doing a wide choice of sketches and paintings, and leaving the client to make the final decision as to which ones he wants to use. Alton Manning apparently knows these islands well, so he should be quite capable of choosing for himself the illustrations he needs for his own book.'

Without the help of his interfering nephew, her glacial look added, and she tensed as she waited for Brook to argue, but his reaction was as unexpected as the man himself. He said smoothly, 'That lets us both off the hook, then, doesn't it?'

Reaching down, he removed her pad and pencil from her suddenly nerveless fingers, and slipped them back into her portfolio. Tucking the latter into his briefcase, and his other hand through her arm, he urged her back along the path to where the driver was waiting to return them to the jetty.

'Come on, we've both done our stint of work for the day. Now it's time to play.'

# CHAPTER FOUR

SHE was playing with fire.

Kit thrust the thought from her angrily. Maggie had told her she must learn to play again. There could be no harm in her enjoying the experience, could there?

Swimming with Brook through the warm blue water galvanised feelings into life which she had thought to be long dead. Kit thrilled to the challenge as they raced each other until her arms tired, while he showed no signs of flagging, but, quick to notice her slow-down, he slowed too, and they idled together, exploring the clear depths that lay beneath their floating forms.

Brook anchored the yacht in a wide bay, and they dived from its rail, and Kit's skin tingled to the sensuous feel of sliding through the surface warmth to the much cooler depths below.

It tingled with an entirely different feeling when Brook, diving beside her, reached out his hand to grasp her own, and guide her to where

a shoal of brilliantly coloured fish swam like
tiny, mobile flowers through a coral garden.

'Something else for you to add to your
sketch-book,' he suggested when they surfaced, and Kit responded breathlessly,

'I didn't have enough time to take in how
they looked. I couldn't hold my breath for long
enough to get more than a quick glimpse. I'm
a bit out of practice,' she understated.

'I've got some snorkelling gear on the yacht.
Let's use it, and go back for a longer look.'

'I've never been snorkelling.' Kit looked
doubtful.

'I'll show you how.'

He unearthed the equipment from one of the
lockers, and commanded Kit to, 'Sit still, while
I fit this mask on you.'

For the second time that day, his hand
stroked the hair back, away from her face. She
quivered under his touch, but if Brook noticed
he gave no sign, and his voice was calm and
impersonal as he said, 'There's no need for you
to hold your breath. Breathe in and out
normally.'

It was not the mask which was making her
hold her breath, but the reassurance that Brook
had mistaken the cause of the sharp intake
steadied Kit, only to make her gasp again when
he finally removed the mask from her face and

added, 'Before we go over the side again, go down into the cabin and rub some sun-barrier cream on your *derrière*.'

'On my *what*?'

Kit gave him an incredulous stare, and her ready colour came and went, but Brook was adamant.

'I'm not joking. When you've got your face underwater, watching fish, the other end of you will be near the surface, and it can get badly sunburned, even through shallow water—which would be a pity.'

His appreciative look heightened Kit's colour still further, but to her relief he did not pursue the point, only explaining, 'It's politely called duck burn, and if you have to eat your meals standing up for the next day or two Lois will have some harsh things to say to me for allowing it to happen.'

'I can't bear the thought of you being shouted at by Lois.' Kit laughed at the unlikely vision of Brook cowering before a wrathful hostess, but she scampered down to the cabin nevertheless, and emerged a few minutes later with the vital protection well rubbed in.

Brook turned from where he had been lounging against the rail, waiting for her. 'You look different when you laugh.'

She felt different, more alive than she had been for months. Maggie had been right, as usual. Kit submitted to having the face mask refitted, feeling the now familiar tingle as Brook's fingers brushed against her cheeks, and wondered nervily why the barrier cream she had already rubbed into her face seemed to be no protection against the heat of his touch.

She followed him back into the water, grateful for the protection of the mask to hide her expression, but her senses, heightened by the small, intimate contact, were so alive to Brook swimming beside her that the coloured fish, and the mysterious coral branches, became a mere background blur, and when she surfaced again beside him she doubted if she would be able to remember enough of the underwater world she had just left to sketch more than a general impression.

They dried off under the deck awning, parted briefly to change back into cottons, and came together again to eat the delicious picnic which Brook produced with a flourish from out of the yacht's galley. The bite of iced fruit juice cooled Kit's throat, and drew from her the surprised comment, 'You're as well equipped as a hotel. This is cordon bleu.'

'The yacht *is* my hotel, when I'm on business trips. I find it more convenient to have an independent base that is completely mobile.'

Brook would always be independent, Kit thought, but she allowed it to pass, and he went on, 'Alton uses the vessel as well, whenever he wants a hideaway to allow him to write in peace, without interruption. A good many of his books have been written on this deck.'

'Nice to have a refuge, without having the bother of its upkeep.'

'I owe Alton that. He was my guardian when I was small. He and my aunt brought me up, after my parents were both killed in a car crash.'

How small had he been when tragedy struck? Kit wondered. And had the young Brook hurt, as she had hurt, and still did? She surveyed him surreptitiously from under her lashes. It was difficult to detect the small, vulnerable child in the wealthy, successful and supremely confident man, but deep inside he might still be lurking there, somewhere. Kit felt suddenly glad that Brook had had caring relatives to turn to in his hour of need. When she most needed her own parents, they were half a world away, immersed in their latest dig.

Silence fell while they ate, and watched a distant liner cruising majestically across the horizon.

'They're not coming over to our island,' Kit said lazily, unaware of the 'our', and of the satisfaction in her voice which earned her a sharp glance from Brook, who answered,

'They don't see the real islands, only the carefully chosen tourist bits. Most of the passengers prefer to carry their own world along with them, when they come on holiday. They're afraid to leave it behind, in case it upsets their preconceived notions. They're afraid of the truth.'

He pushed aside the small trolley which held the debris of their meal, and rolled over to face Kit. 'With me, you'll see the islands just as they are, the good, and the not so good. Are you afraid, I wonder?'

His eyes were a challenge. They bored into Kit's, grey pools which held their secrets, unlike the warm blue waters they had swum in together, which had so generously shared their depths with the snorkelling visitors. Kit had a sudden urge to unlock Brook's secrets, to find the young, vulnerable child hidden deep inside the man. And if she found him, what then? Was she afraid? She took refuge in evasion.

'I left my life behind me, and came to find the real islands.'

She had come to find herself as well, but that was her secret, and was not to be revealed.

Suddenly nervous in case the all-seeing eyes might penetrate it, she jumped to her feet.

'Shouldn't we be getting back? Lois will be wondering where we've got to.' She glanced at her wristwatch, gave it a sharper scrutiny, and then shook it disbelievingly. 'It can't really be that time? It must be hours since we first set out. I didn't realise how the time had flown.' The second hand continued to circle remorselessly, so the watch could not have stopped.

'Forget your watch.' Brook flowed upright, and, reaching across, he turned the dial of her watch to the front of her wrist, so that the figures on it were hidden. 'Use island time instead,' he said.

'Island time? What's that?'

'The sun tells you when it's time to get up. Hunger tells you when it's time to eat.' Brook paused for a telling moment, and his eyes fired with that strange inner glow which Kit had noticed in them before. He took a step closer to her, and, reaching out, he drew her masterfully into his arms. 'The moon tells you when it's time to make love,' he finished softly.

Time ceased to matter.

Kit was conscious only of the hard, demanding pressure of Brook's mouth exploring her own, of the quick hunger of her lips in response, which had been starved for too long,

and had never tasted food like this. She fought
to bring them under control, but their need was
stronger than her will, and they pursed under
his kiss. In vain she rallied her voice to her
defence.

'Brook, no...please...'

'You're contradicting yourself,' he murmured, and the laughter in his voice mocked
her, stinging her into action.

She began to struggle in his arms. The fear
was real enough now, cutting through her like
a knife, but for all the impression she made she
might as well have tried to struggle against iron
bars as against the bondage of his arms.

His only response to her protest was to draw
her closer, moulding her to him the better for
his lips to trace the gentle contours of her
cheeks, and move on along the slender jawline
to where a pulse throbbed to a rhythm that was
wilder than any reggae beat, and more insistent
than calypso.

Kit was breathless when Brook finally let her
go. She felt shaken to the core by her own unexpected reaction, as much as by Brook's
caress. Seeking his vulnerability, she had only
succeeded in revealing the depths of her own,
and the fear she felt was as much of herself as
it was of him.

His kisses challenged her to live again, to *feel* again, and feeling was something she had tried desperately to shut out of her life since Paul. She was only too well aware that the lack of feeling had shown itself in her work. Her paintings had become brittle and defensive, denying viewers access to their hidden meaning. Some of the more arty types looked wise, and commented that Kit Fielding's style was changing, becoming more mature.

Others, more perceptive, wondered.

'Let go... You'll never know peace until you do,' Maggie had warned her, and wearily Kit wished she knew how.

It took one of Lois's young pupils to show her the way. He appeared one day about a week later, while Kit was sitting on the veranda with Lois and Jesse and Brook, doing nothing in particular. It had been a week of hectic activity, and Lois had declared a holiday for them all.

'School's out for the week, and even machines need a rest sometimes,' she had told the others sternly, and reluctantly Kit had laid aside her sketching materials.

Each day Brook had called to take her to yet another island. Kit despised herself for the eager anticipation with which she watched for the yacht to appear, cruising across the bay like some exotic taxi, but each morning found her glued to the veranda rail, searching the horizon for the first sign of the vessel to appear.

She made the weak excuse to herself that she was here to see the islands, and Brook and his yacht were merely a means to that end, but the excitement remained, and with it a growing unease.

She had no complaints about the results so far as her work was concerned. Her portfolio grew fat as she worked feverishly each evening, translating the best of the day's sketches into paintings, unwilling to let the colours or the sharpness of her impressions fade by even a few hours, before they became overlaid by new ones the next day.

Jesse had been right in his claim that each island was unique. Kit viewed with amazement the French sophistication of Martinique, boasting shops that might have been whisked straight from a Paris boulevard, and brooded on the lot of the inhabitants of a shanty town on an island less well endowed, but whose people still seemed to find it easy to smile.

'The collapse of the oil prices hit the economy hard,' Brook commented, seeing her dismay, 'but they're fighting back.'

'Anyone who can smile like that deserves to win.'

He persuaded Kit to sample fine wine and delicate pastries in an upmarket restaurant, and then took her to share a meal of spiced fish and rice, washed down with milk drunk straight from a newly beheaded coconut, while sitting on a sun-baked rock chatting to workers from the nearby grove, and of the two meals Kit enjoyed the latter more.

Brook seemed to be accepted, and completely at his ease, in both worlds, she noticed. The man was like a chameleon, taking on the colourings of his surroundings. He had promised to show her the good, and the not so good, and he kept his word with a thoroughness which made Kit accuse him of malice aforethought.

'Did you *have* to choke me with fumes?' She gagged on the sulphurous air of an evil-looking lake.

'You said you wanted to see the real islands. Don't despise one of the globe's biggest sources of asphalt,' was all the sympathy she got.

Kit gave the black, tarry surface of the lake an ungrateful look, and promptly forgave it some time later when even stronger smells competed from the butchery section of a downtown market, and, she decided rucfully, won hands down.

'You're doing this just to be spiteful,' she hissed at him furiously. 'Take me away, anywhere, I don't care where; it's ghastly.'

'Forget your nose.'

'I wish I could, I——'

'Stand still, and use your ears instead.'

Brook drew her to stand against him, holding her still so that she had no option but to take in the myriad sounds of the market, making her experience them for herself as he had insisted all along that she must. She wriggled in his grasp impatiently.

'I can't hear anything different...' she began, and then stopped.

A woman's voice, soft and yet clear, rose over the bustle of the market in a snatch of song. The sound grew louder as other voices joined in, and soon it seemed as if the whole market was singing. Kit listened enthralled, the smells forgotten.

Without realising what she was doing, she beat time with her hands, carried along on a magic carpet of sound. The woven straw hat which Brook had insisted she must wear in the sun slipped unnoticed to the back of her head, revealing her face alight with pleasure. Faces turned and smiled at her. Kit smiled right back, unaware of Brook watching her, wondering what, or who, had put the shadows into the

clear hazel eyes of this girl, which in moments
of forgetfulness such as this, and increasingly
during the last few days, could brim with delighted laughter, transforming the elfin face.

The singing died away as suddenly as it
began. Shoppers returned to bargaining with
the traders, the smell of the meat reasserted
itself. Brook drew Kit away. 'Time to go.'

'You knew about the singing.'

'Yes.'

'You didn't tell me.'

'It would have spoilt it for you if I had. To
really appreciate it, you've got to hear it for
yourself, out of the blue.'

Brook was right, of course. He always was,
and his rightness rankled, and soured the experience for her anyway. The shadows returned
to brood in her gaze that evening as Kit lay
back in her chair and decided that a long, cool
glass of fruit juice was no substitute for a
sketch-block and pencil as a defence against
intrusive thoughts, which against her will
seemed to be centring more on Brook than on
the islands he was taking her to visit.

Two young schoolboys scampering up the
path towards the house provided a welcome
distraction. 'It looks as if you've got visitors,'
Kit smiled at Lois, and her hostess groaned.

'Just when I'm supposed to be on holiday,' she complained.

'Tell them to go away.' Jesse sank deeper into his chair, and stretched out his feet to rest them on the veranda rail.

'I mustn't,' his wife answered. 'I told them to let me have their homework as soon as they'd finished it, so that I can mark their books during the holiday. I can't turn them away now.'

A rhythmic rattling sound came from something which the children appeared to be shaking in their hands, and their teacher relaxed with a sigh of relief.

'From the sound of that,' she said hopefully, 'they won't want to hang about for long. They'll have band practice to go to afterwards.'

'What is it they're rattling?' Kit asked interestedly, grasping eagerly at the antidote to her own unwelcome thoughts.

'They're shack shacks. Dried seed pods, which make a nice noise. The junior boys at the school have formed a shack-shack band of their own. They're doing quite well, and it provides them with a nice interest outside of school hours. At the moment they're busy practising for carnival. I wish they'd work as hard at their lessons,' she smiled, and raised her voice to call out to her young visitors, 'Come on up, boys. We're on the veranda.'

She accepted the work they had prepared, and rewarded them with a glass of lemonade each, and they settled happily on the floor at her feet to drink it, chatting away with the unselfconscious friendliness that Kit had learned to expect from the islanders of all ages.

'Do you want to be in a band, when you leave school?' she asked, and the younger of the two shook his head emphatically.

'I want to have a boat, and be a scientist, like Jesse.'

'Having a boat won't make you a scientist,' his older companion declared scornfully, but the younger boy was not to be deterred.

'I know it won't. But it'll sure make me humming-bird happy!'

Kit joined in the laughter as the children finished their lemonade, and went on their way, but her eyes were soft on the two small figures as they ran off down the garden path towards the beach, energetically shaking their shack shacks.

'I hope he gets his wish,' she murmured.

Brook regarded her quizzically. 'Which one? To be a scientist, or to have a boat of his own?'

'Neither. I just hope he'll be humming-bird happy.'

Let them always be as happy as they are now, she wished silently as the young voices floated back to the grown-ups on the veranda, arguing amicably over the rhythm they were shaking out of their seed pods.

'My beat is better than yours,' the older one claimed, and his companion shouted back,

'No, it isn't. Mine's good, too. I've heard it played on the radio.'

'Your beat is yesterday's, man. Mine is new.'

Kit's ears could detect no difference, even if her mind had been capable of registering the beat. The child's innocent words seemed to bounce round and round in her mind, like an echo of the shack shack itself.

Yesterday's man . . .

She took out the comma, and changed the emphasis, and felt a burden lift from off her shoulders.

Yesterday's man was Paul.

The children's voices faded into silence, and Kit leaned back in her chair and closed her eyes, and quietly let the hurt slip into the past, where it belonged. She would never be quite the same again, after Paul. The experience had matured her. She was older, if not wiser.

But at last she was free.

Unconsciously she shook her head, rejecting the next thought which tracked unbidden across her mind to follow the first.

Would there be a tomorrow's man for her?

# CHAPTER FIVE

'YOU must see the carnival, Kit. You haven't lived until you've seen a Caribbean carnival,' Lois returned to the subject with enthusiasm the next morning. 'There'll be steel bands, decorated floats, fancy costumes, jump-ups—oh, absolutely everything!' she exclaimed.

'Jump-ups?' Kit looked her puzzlement.

'You hear the music, and you jump up and dance.'

'It sounds wonderful. And colourful. Just ideal for sketching,' Kit responded eagerly. Now that she was rid at last of her burden, new experiences took on a brighter hue.

Brook promptly clouded it with a firm, 'It's no use you just looking on. Leave your sketchbook behind, and join in. You can't get the flavour of food unless you taste it.'

He was determined to make her experience in person every single thing she painted. Kit threw him a look of rebellion. She had been engaged by Brook's uncle, not by Brook, and he had absolutely no right to direct her work in this authoritarian manner. If the author trusted her judgement, that was good enough. The fact that her own professional instincts agreed with Brook made his manner rankle even more.

New experiences were the breath of life to any artist. She had only tasted one 'food' that had so sickened her that she had vowed never to try it again. There would be no tomorrow's man for her. But that was a secret which she did not intend to share, least of all with Brook. As for the carnival . . . Her hostile eyes clashed with the open challenge in Brook's, but before the encounter could ignite Jesse butted in, 'Why don't we all go? Everything on the island stops for carnival, so Brook and I won't be able to get any work done for the next few days, even if we want to, and Lois has got time off school.'

'That's a great idea.' His wife took up the suggestion enthusiastically, and Brook added, 'I've got an even better one.'

He would have, Kit thought sourly, but she remained silent as he went on, 'Why don't we all move on to the yacht for a few days? That way, we can follow the carnival events round the island without having to waste time coming back to the house each evening.'

He received the couple's eager acceptance with a satisfied nod, and, 'That's settled, then,' and seemed to take her own compliance for granted, Kit fumed, but a rising tide of excitement fought with her resentment. To live on the *Dolphin*, even for a few days, would be an experience never to be forgotten. How Maggie's eyes would widen, when she told her about it! And the presence of Lois and Jesse would act as an effective buffer between herself and Brook.

Lois lent her a small suitcase. 'You won't need to take much with you. Something to lounge about in during the day and a nice dress for the evenings will do.'

Kit packed with a mixture of apprehension and excitement. If Brook had his way, she would not be doing much lounging, and as an act of last-minute defiance she threw in her sketching materials and small portfolio. Together, they made the silent statement that if Brook was on holiday she herself was not, and he could not argue with that.

He did not try. Brook's method was more direct, and devastatingly effective. He kept Kit so busy that she had neither the time nor the energy left with which to sketch. He entered the *Dolphin* in the inter-island yacht race, and pressed Kit into service as his crew.

'I can't. I *won't*,' she panicked. 'I don't know a sail from an oar.'

'You can. You *must*. If you——'

# Discover
# FREE BOOKS
### AND
# FREE GIFTS
## From Mills & Boon

**As a special introduction to
Mills & Boon Romances we will send you:**

**16 FREE Mills & Boon Romances**
plus a **FREE TEDDY** and **MYSTERY GIFT** when you
return this card.

But first - just for fun - see if you can find and circle four
hidden words in the puzzle.

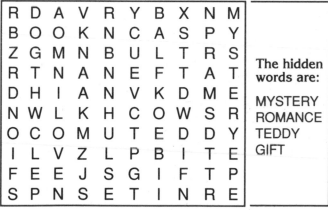

| R | D | A | V | R | Y | B | X | N | M |
|---|---|---|---|---|---|---|---|---|---|
| B | O | O | K | N | C | A | S | P | Y |
| Z | G | M | N | B | U | L | T | R | S |
| R | T | N | A | N | E | F | T | A | T |
| D | H | I | A | N | V | K | D | M | E |
| N | W | L | K | H | C | O | W | S | R |
| O | C | O | M | U | T | E | D | Y | Y |
| I | L | V | Z | L | P | B | I | T | E |
| F | E | E | J | S | G | I | F | T | P |
| S | P | N | S | E | T | I | N | R | E |

**The hidden
words are:**

MYSTERY
ROMANCE
TEDDY
GIFT

Now turn over to claim your
**FREE BOOKS AND GIFTS**

# Free Books Certificate

**Yes** Please send me FREE and without obligation 16 specially selected Mills & Boon Romances, together with my FREE teddy and mystery gift. Please also reserve a special Reader Service subscription for me. If I decide to subscribe, I shall receive 16 superb Romances every month for just £28.80, postage and packing FREE. If I decide not to subscribe I shall write to you within 10 days. The FREE books and gifts will be mine to keep in any case. I understand that I am under no obligation whatsoever. I may cancel or suspend my subscription at any time simply by writing to you. I am over the age of 18.

11A3R

**FREE TEDDY**

**MYSTERY GIFT**

Ms/Mrs/Miss/Mr

Address

Postcode

Signature

Mills & Boon
Reader Service
FREEPOST
P.O. Box 236
Croydon
Surrey CR9 9EL

NO
STAMP
NEEDED

'—don't taste the food, you won't get the flavour,' Kit chanted, tasting instead the sourness of defeat.

Unaware of the barbed undercurrents, Jesse urged, 'Never mind if you've never done it before, Kit. It's an experience not to be missed.'

It was one experience she could have lived without, Kit decided raggedly, as the flavours which Brook had promised came thick and fast, not all of them palatable.

The starter's pistol exploded in her ears like an evil omen, and Kit grabbed desperately at the nearest hand-hold to keep on her feet as the sails billowed, and Brook swung the yacht in a wide arc, leaning it over at an angle that made her fearfully certain that the vessel must turn turtle on top of them.

By what seemed a miracle it righted itself and sped on, with other, similar vessels racing neck and neck, skilful to gain every second's advantage over their rivals to help them to win the prestigious cup. It was all a far cry from the quiet cruising which was all Kit had experienced of yacht life so far.

Curt orders reached her from the cockpit, and she longed to mutiny and shout back, Do it yourself. I quit! But there was nowhere to quit to, except over the rail into the water. A harassed glance warned her that the shoreline was a lot too far away to swim for it, and, besides, the other yachts were gaining on them. Passing them . . .

In desperation Kit forced her unaccustomed hands to the tasks which Brook demanded of them, and she could have wept with frustration when, in spite of her efforts, three of their rivals forged ahead of the *Dolphin*. Rage and disappointment, and a helpless feeling of guilt at her own inadequacy, turned Kit's anger on to Brook, for subjecting her to such an ordeal, instead of crewing with Jesse, the skilful, knowledgeable Jesse, who knew every inch of these waters, and who, with Brook, would have taken the *Dolphin* across the finishing line in triumph.

They sailed across in fourth place, honourable enough considering her own complete inexperience of sailing, and a credit to Brook's expert handling of his vessel with a completely green crew, but Kit was not to be consoled. She felt limp with heat and nervous exhaustion, and dejection and anger assailed her in about equal measure.

'It serves you right,' she spat at Brook. 'You should have taken Jesse instead.'

'If I had, you wouldn't have known what it was like to take part in a yacht race.'

'I didn't need to know. Alton's book doesn't mention inter-island races.'

Brook had done this thing simply to show his authority, and humiliate her, and she would not forgive him for that.

'What would you call the scene where the coastguard cutter chased the villain from island to island, before he was finally arrested?' he asked her mildly.

A race by any other name, but Kit felt she would die rather than admit it. She clamped her lips together, refusing to answer, and the dance in the yacht club afterwards did nothing to soothe her feelings.

Her companions seemed to know and be known by everybody there, and Kit found herself welcomed into the midst of their friends with the warm-heartedness which was typical of the islands, but the innocent commiserations on the loss of the race rubbed salt into the already sore wound of her pride.

'What happened, Brook? You won last year, and you came second the year before that...'

'*I* happened,' Kit burst out bitterly, and they laughed and consoled her,

'Don't take it to heart. The race is only a fun thing. By next year you'll be as good a crewman as the rest.'

By this time next year she would be a long way away from both Brook and his yacht, and it could not come too soon for her, Kit glowered inwardly. She sat tensely and without appetite through the festive dinner, which progressed through a number of speeches, and ended with the presentation of the winner's trophy.

He held it aloft in triumph, to uproarious applause from his fellow diners, and the glitter of the silver cup seemed to mock Kit. No matter how kind the others had been, they could not take away the sting of defeat, and it was an inescapable fact that, but for her own fumbling inexperience, it could have been Brook standing there, holding aloft the silver cup.

Because of her he had lost the race, and only Kit knew about his other, hidden victory over herself in forcing her to crew for him. That cup held a bitter draught for her, which she found more difficult to swallow than the loss of a mere race. The applause died away, and Jesse heaved a sigh of relief and said, 'Thank goodness for that. Now we can get dancing.'

They rose along with the other diners, and made their way towards the source of softly played music from another room, and Kit's tension increased with every reluctant step she took. This was the moment she had most dreaded, the moment when she must dance again, for the first time since Paul. How would she cope, if the band played 'their' tune?

Kit's mind raced in circles, trying ineffectually to think up some plausible excuse to release her from the ordeal, but nothing presented itself, and Jesse asked with a smile, as he led his wife into the first dance, 'Save the next one for me, Kit?'

Kit managed an answering smile, which instantly faded when Brook put his arm about her waist, and, drawing her to him, murmured in her ear, 'Shall we dance?'

The glint in his eyes mocked her reluctance without knowing its cause, and the firmness of his hold turned his request into an order which Kit had no choice but to obey since she could not extricate herself without an undignified struggle.

Her heart raced as her feet automatically followed Brook's lead, but it was not memories of Paul which made her pulses throb. The discovery should have come as a relief, and instead it added to her tension to discover that it was Brook, and not her late husband, who accelerated her heartbeat until it became a pain in her throat.

Her heightened senses quivered into a vivid awareness of him, like delicately tuned radio antennae picking up messages which they did not want to receive, and—she caught a small, dismayed breath—perhaps even transmitting similar messages back.

The vibes which flowed from Brook seemed to travel without conscious effort on his part, which made them all the more deadly. They were like fierce probes, seeking out her vulnerability. Kit's feet missed a step, and she stumbled, and Brook's arm tightened round her, making her confusion worse.

She turned scarlet, and then white, and her mind reeled. A loud roaring started in her ears, and she heard Brook's voice sharp and incisive, penetrating a thickening fog which threatened to overwhelm her.

'What's the matter? Are you feeling faint?'

'Yes...no...' She could not explain how she was feeling. The turmoil of her senses defied rational explanation. She managed, 'It's hot in here...'

Of course it was hot. What else could it be, on a tropical island? The absurdity of her answer steadied Kit slightly, and she grasped at it as an excuse to save herself. She said as firmly as she could manage, 'I'll take a walk outside for a minute or two, and cool off.'

'You mustn't go outside at this hour. The no-see-'ums will get you. Sit here, and wait for me. I'll go and fetch you an iced drink.'

Brook pressed her firmly down on to a chair, and Kit sat resentfully. No-see-'ums indeed! Indignation boiled in her, and she glared at Brook's retreating back as he headed towards the bar to get her drink. How dared he patronise her with silly superstitions, like a grown-up frightening a child into obedience with the threat of a bogey-man? Temper proved a quick restorative.

Brook could keep his drink! And, as for her waiting for him, she had better things to do. Kit jumped to her feet defiantly. She would take her walk outside, no-see-'ums notwithstanding. Whatever they were, they could not be any more dangerous than Brook himself, she thought with an inward grin, and made for the nearest door.

A boardwalk landing-stage beckoned, and she turned along it, careful to keep the heels of her sandals from catching in the spaces between the planks. A turned ankle would give Brook the ideal opportunity to say, I told you so.

Water shone below her as she strolled between rows of moored yachts quietly bobbing at rest on either side of her after their recent exertions in the race. The only sounds were the gentle lapping of water against the hulls, and the rhythmic tapping of equipment against the

now denuded masts. Kit drew in a deep breath,
and allowed herself to relax. There was no one
else to be seen. Presumably everybody was in
the clubhouse enjoying the party, and she savoured the luxury of her stolen solitude.

Her smile held a hint of malice as she pic-
tured Brook returning with her drink, to find
her missing. The boot would be on the other
foot, for once, she thought with satisfaction.
He would assume that she had gone to the
powder-room, and he would wait around for
her, expecting her to return at any moment.
The ice in her drink would be long melted
before she did, she determined grimly.

She sauntered slowly to the end of the
landing-stage, taking her time, and was turning
to make her unhurried way back again when
the exposed parts of her skin began to itch.
Within seconds, Kit was rubbing herself fran-
tically. Her bare arms, her shoulders and back
above the scooped neckline of her dress, her
legs, all felt as if they were on fire.

Forgetting her resolution to make Brook
wait, she accelerated back towards the clubhouse. She needed the powder-room now, with
a vengeance. It must be something she had
eaten at dinner. There could be no other explanation for the sudden torment which spread
across her skin like an invading army. Her mind

vied with her hurrying feet for speed, going back over every detail of the dinner menu. She had been so tense that she had hardly noticed what it was she had eaten, but if she was to find an antidote to the now desperate discomfort she had to know the cause.

Starters? She remembered those. Melon was harmless enough. Main course? The itching increased, and she broke into a run. She must find Lois, and fast.

She burst back through the doorway from which she had only recently escaped, and collided with her quarry. Lois exclaimed, 'Kit! I've been looking all over for you. Where did you get to? You weren't in the powder-room.'

'I've been out for a walk, along the landing-stage.'

'Not by the water, at this time in the evening?' Lois's expression registered almost comical dismay. 'Oh, Kit! The no-see-'ums...'

'Not you, too!' Kit exclaimed impatiently. 'I'm in no mood to listen to superstitions. My skin's on fire. It must be something I ate at dinner that I'm allergic to.'

'It isn't what you've eaten, it's what's eaten you.' Lois took her arm, and tut-tutted over the scratch marks. 'No-see-'ums are tiny insects. They're so small you literally can't see them. You don't even know they're there until they bite you. You know all about it then, though. For all they're so tiny, they've got a bite that itches worse than a mosquito's. Oh, you poor dear,' she said as Kit rubbed herself frenziedly, 'Brook should have warned you.'

'I did,' Brook drawled, 'but she didn't listen, so the only thing to do was to let her find out for herself.'

He had guessed she had gone outside, after he had warned her not to, and he had let her go without bothering to explain what he meant, knowing what the consequences would be.

'You're cruel,' Kit burst out. How could he do this to her? Suddenly, humiliatingly, the shiny bubble of her defiance burst, and she wanted to burst into tears. She held them back valiantly, but the glitter in her eyes hated Brook for his callous behaviour. He met her glare with an unrepentant,

'The next time, maybe you'll heed me.'

It was impossible not to heed him. Brook was a man you could not ignore if you wanted to. You either loved him, or loathed him, and she loathed him, Kit told herself fiercely.

Lois glanced from one to the other of their set faces, and took Kit by the arm. 'Come into the powder-room with me. They'll have something there which will take away the irritation. It's standard first aid round these parts, although mostly it's only used for visitors. The locals know better than to risk offering themselves as targets in the evening, at least on the leeward side of the islands.'

She should have known better, known better than to get tangled with Brook in the first place, Kit chastised herself miserably.

If only she had refused his offer of a lift that day at the restaurant. Fate had not only dealt her Metro a cruel blow, it had dealt her one too, in the shape of Brook, and that was crueller still. Almost as cruel as the man himself.

Kit subsided into a chair in the blessed privacy of the powder-room, while Lois rummaged in a cupboard and came out with a sizeable bottle of something which smelled nice when she unscrewed the stopper.

'Ooh, that's bliss,' Kit breathed her gratitude as her friend unzipped the back of her dress, and applied the lotion generously even to the bits that did not itch.

'Just in case there are any of the little beasties still hanging around looking for a meal,' she teased a smile back to Kit's face.

'It's magic,' acknowledged her relieved patient. 'My skin is beginning to feel bearable again now. Thank goodness there was some lotion handy.'

Now that her body was restored to reasonable comfort, Kit's mind clicked back into gear, and she grasped at the opportunity to extricate herself from at least a few hours of Brook's unwanted company on the following day.

'I think I'll miss out on that beach barbecue Brook was talking about for tomorrow evening. I've no notion to invite another aerial attack.'

Brook could keep his barbecued meal, as well as his iced drink, she thought waspishly, only to have Lois block her avenue of escape with an assurance which was meant to be comforting, and was just the opposite.

'There's no need for you to miss out on the fun. You'll be fine. The barbecue is being held on a beach on the windward side of the island, for that very reason. The wind keeps the insects away,' she explained. 'You won't be bothered by no-see-'ums at the barbecue, and the smoke from the burnt bits helps as well,' she laughed.

No-see-'ums did not bother her half so much as Brook, Kit thought raggedly. He was larger than life and a lot more difficult to combat. There was no antidote to his stings. They penetrated deeper, and left behind an irritation more lasting than any insect bite.

'How are the bites?' Brook enquired the next morning when they all forgathered on the yacht's deck for breakfast.

Kit regarded him suspiciously. His voice was even, displaying only the consideration of a courteous host enquiring after the well-being of his guest.

His eyes laughed at her.

She bridled; her return look matched the ice in her glass of fruit juice, and her voice held a bite of its own as she retorted, 'Gone,' and added through clenched teeth, 'Thanks to Lois.'

Her unforgiving glare said, No thanks to you, and the laughter spread to Brook's lips.

'If you suffer from your mistakes, you won't make them again.'

The knuckles of Kit's fingers showed suddenly white as they tightened convulsively round her glass. She had suffered—how she had suffered—from her mistake with Paul, and she would not make that one again.

'Too right, I won't,' she answered tightly, and she meant one thing, and Brook meant another, and his eyes narrowed on her set face, with all the laughter gone from them.

'Cool down,' he drawled. 'Bad temper is no luggage to carry about with you at a carnival.'

He was accusing *her* of bad temper! He showed absolutely no remorse for being the

cause of it. Kit's even tighter grip threatened
the life of the fragile tumbler, and Lois saved
it from extinction just in time by remarking
kindly, 'I'm glad the lotion worked. Nothing
must get in the way of you enjoying your very
first Caribbean carnival.'

Nothing, and nobody, Kit vowed. Not insects. Not memories of Paul. *Not Brook*. I
won't let any of them spoil it for me, she told
herself sturdily. It might be the only time she
would ever see a carnival in this home of car-
nivals. They had all tried their cruel best to
spoil things for her. It was up to her to make
sure they did not succeed.

It proved to be easier than she had imagined
to relax and join in the fun. A steel band struck
up a lively tune from the shore, setting her feet
tapping. Colourful costumes began to make
their appearance on the road leading from the
tiny harbour where Brook had anchored the
yacht for the night, and when he called out,
'Time to go, folks. Take to the boat,' Kit
laughed and scrambled down the ladder with
the others, and joined Lois in the *Dolphin*'s
tender for Jesse and Brook to row them ashore.

On land, all was hectic activity. There was
no time to remember, no time in which to think,
only to do, and to feel—to experience the carnival, just as Brook intended her to. Music

poured from the open doorways of cafés, vibrating the sun-warmed air, and the light breeze stirred the gaily coloured bunting as if it, too, was trying to dance.

Extravagant costumes added even more colour, mute evidence of the skills that had gone into their making. Floats rumbled past, garlanded with flowers, and headed by a spectacular bower carrying the carnival queen. The girl was ravishingly beautiful. Kit longed to do a painting of her, but her equipment was on the yacht, and she forgot the urge as the queen for the day tossed blossoms to the crowd. People grasped at them eagerly as they fell, and Brook said, 'They're supposed to bring luck for the year, until the next carnival.' He reached up deft fingers and plucked one in flight, and turned to tuck it behind Kit's ear. 'In the meantime, it will help to keep the hair out of your eyes,' he smiled.

His own had not missed her habitual, nervous gesture, and she went rigid as his fingers caught up some of the silky strands, and plaited them round the blossom's slender stem.

'You should always wear a flower in your hair,' he told her. 'It suits you.'

'They—they—won't stay in. At least, not for me,' Kit stammered, unable to meet his searching look.

This one would stay in, because Brook had bidden it. The movement of her head drifted its perfume across her nostrils, heavy and honey-sweet, soothing as an opiate to her jangled nerves, urging her to let go and play, just as Maggie had said.

Jesse called out a cheery, 'It's a jump-up. Let's go,' as a float bearing a steel band drew a crowd of dancing couples in its wake with the magnetism of a pied piper.

People clicked fingers and twitched hips in time to the insistent beat of the music, and Brook released Kit's hair and spun her round. With his hands on her hips he turned her in front of him and commanded, 'Shimmy, woman. Shimmy!'

His hands propelled her forward. The perfume from the flower lured her on, and, caught up by the beat of the music, Kit's unaccustomed hips twirled in the movements of the strange, erotic dance, as if she had been doing it all her life.

Brook's hands were an electric link between them as he danced behind her, and Kit became an extension of them, impelled by their thrust, brought to life by the vibrant life which flowed from Brook's hold, letting go with a thoroughness that forgot the past, and left only the present, and blinded her to what the future might hold.

She was panting and laughing when Brook finally drew her aside from the dance and commanded, 'That's enough, for now. You're out of breath,' and added as he pulled her to face him, 'You look different when you laugh.'

He had said the same thing once before, on the yacht, but here she had no convenient snorkel mask to hide her expression.

Live dangerously, Maggie had advised.

In a sudden surge of recklessness, Kit lifted her unprotected face to Brook, knowing that he was going to kiss her, telling herself that she did not care. What was a kiss in the middle of a carnival, with the sun shining, and the steel band playing, and countless other couples doing exactly the same thing?

This was carnival day, *her* day, and Brook was just one small part of it.

His kiss made him the largest part. It exploded through Kit's senses with the force of a million shooting stars, regardless of the fact that it was broad daylight. It lasted seconds in time, and a lifetime in sensation, and blotted out the myriad sights and sounds which she had come to experience.

Kit was aware only of the heat of Brook's lips covering her own, burning, demanding, of the heady sweetness of the flower which he had plaited in her hair. The rich, honey scent roused her to the ecstasy of his kiss, and drugged her to its danger, and stifled the small voice inside her which struggled to warn her.

For, in trying to repay Brook for that first, disastrous lunch, if she was not careful, the coin she used would be her own heart.

# CHAPTER SIX

'LET'S take it easy today.' Lois stretched lazy arms above her head the next morning, as Brook and his guests lounged at their ease on the deck over an early coffee.

Lethargy had set in after the hectic activities of the day before, and no one seemed to be inclined to exert themselves beyond the needs of desultory conversation.

'What did you think of a Caribbean carnival, Kit?' Jesse asked, and Kit answered slowly,

'It was—unforgettable.'

Was it the carnival that was unforgettable, or was it being with Brook that had made it so? Nervously Kit dodged the question. Her mind was in a turmoil, and she wanted time to think, and to adjust.

Time was the one thing which was being denied to her. There was no way in which she could escape Brook's company. Ruefully she acknowledged a fellow feeling with the islands. She, too, felt as if she had been hit by a hurricane.

She wished she could blame the cause of her riotous emotions on the island's potent white rum, and knew that the far more potent cause was Brook himself. Her eyes brooded over the water, to where the pale crescent of beach marked the site of the barbecue the evening before, towards the clump of palm trees under which they had stood together, and kissed. Only the silver light of the moon was missing this morning—the moon that said when it was time to make love. Island time... The moon had been hugely brilliant, last night.

'Right on cue,' Brook congratulated its appearance, and moulded Kit to him.

She did not try to resist him. She was still on a high from the dancing, and made reckless by the small measure of white rum which Jesse had laced her fruit juice with, and insisted she must taste. Kit took her glass from him doubtfully.

'I'm not used to rum. Won't it make me light-headed on an empty stomach?' She dreaded any loss of self-control while she was in Brook's company; she felt she needed all of her strength in order to combat his.

'The drop I've put in your orange juice won't hurt you,' Jesse reassured her, 'and the barbecue will soon be ready to eat. Rum is a part of the islands, so you ought to taste it at least once.'

Its strength was relative. Kit's unaccustomed palate absorbed the taste, while her body, hungry for the food soon to come, registered more strongly the relaxing warmth which trickled through her veins like liquid fire. It eased away the tensions, and left her instincts in charge of her mind.

They bent her, pliant in Brook's arms, charged by the electric currents which flowed from his hold, and which tempted her unruly tongue into a provocative question. 'On cue for what?'

'Us,' he answered throatily.

Through the protective haze of the rum Kit watched his eyes fire, and knew deep down that she should feel afraid, but fear, like memories, seemed to be part of another world. If someone mentioned Paul to her now, she would have to ask, 'Paul who?' There was only Brook in the whole wide world. Brook, and the big silver moon.

I'm tipsy, she thought, and wanted to giggle, and forgot the urge as Brook's head became a descending silhouette above her, blotting out the now redundant moon. Brook's hands caressed her, rousing in her longings she had tried to forget. His lips laid siege to her own, blurring

the past and the future, and leaving only the
timeless present.

Kit grasped at the present, for that was what
carnival was all about, wasn't it? Everybody
said so...

The barbecued meat they ate afterwards
tasted like the food of the gods, hot and spicy
and delicious, better than any other food she
had eaten before. They ate it from their fingers,
strolling along the waterline together, laughing
as they dodged the waves that, on this
windward side of the island, sent up showers
of spray. But the brisk wind, as Lois had
promised, kept the insects at bay, and, if it un-
settled the waves, it took away nothing from
the magic of the night.

With Brook's arm round her shoulders, Kit
could laugh at the rough sea. He held her close,
and the smooth flow of his strong thigh muscles
as he walked sent tingles through her own, but
in her present state of euphoria Kit only pressed
the closer to him, recklessly savouring the sensations as her tongue had savoured the rum.

Afterwards, when the barbecue was over,
and they all went back again to the yacht, Jesse
and Lois called their goodnights and went
below to their cabin, and Kit and Brook were
left alone on the deck together.

They came to each other's arms as if it was the most natural thing to do, the *only* thing to do, and Brook's voice sounded husky in her ears.

'You're beautiful, Kit . . .'

Nobody had ever called her beautiful before. Her work had warranted the description, but not herself. Paul had always called her cute. Kit savoured this other new sensation as Brook's lips captured her own.

'Kit . . . oh, Kit, I——'

'Don't let's waste time talking.'

Kit reached up and moulded her lips back on to his mouth, begrudging precious seconds spent in any other way, but after a long minute Brook's hands clamped hard on her shoulders, and put her away from him.

'Get below,' he ordered her roughly, 'while I've still got the strength to let you go.'

The hoarseness in his voice was more evident now, and Kit stared up at him bewilderedly.

'No, Brook. Not yet.'

Like a child, she did not want this one perfect day to end. And yet, not like a child, but like a woman. A woman aroused, and eager for love.

Brook was adamant. 'There's tomorrow . . .'

'I don't want tomorrow, I want *now*.' Was she becoming a 'now' person, too? Kit was beyond caring. She choked, 'If you make me go, I'll hate you.'

'I must make you go, because . . .'

She did not wait to hear because of what. With a stifled sob she spun away from his loosened arms, and ran below deck, hating him with a fierce hatred. He was cruel to make her go. Kit blamed the rum, and despised herself, for allowing Brook to draw her on, and then, humiliatingly, rejecting her, and, torn as Kit was between longing and loathing, the shoreline became faintly visible in the first light of the new morning before she eventually dropped off to sleep.

In the hours between, no matter how hard she tried to shut her ears to the sound, Brook's footsteps pacing overhead refused to allow her to rest. Their even tread, backwards and for-wards on the deck above her, became a hyp-notic thing, subjecting his need to the iron discipline of his will, and ignoring her own.

Kit counted frustratedly ten steps towards the wheel house, and ten steps back again. Backwards and forwards, for what seemed to be hours, like a sentry treading the ramparts. Guarding what? Her, or himself?

She wanted to scream out to Brook to stop, and when he finally did, and she heard him come below, she held her breath and waited, but his steps went on, past her cabin door to his own, and the firm click of the latch was like the slamming of his door in her face. With a stifled sob she turned it into the pillow and let the tears flow, and the cool cotton felt damp against her cheek before she finally drifted off into a restless slumber.

She slept late the next morning, and when she emerged she was heavy-eyed and unrefreshed, and felt wearily grateful to Lois that her hostess complained of feeling just the same, so that there was nothing to remark of in her own lethargy.

Kit poured out a cup of strong coffee, and took it to a lounger next to the one Lois was stretched out on. Contrarily, she wanted to stay as far away as possible from Brook this morning. She stole a glance at his face. He showed no signs of his late night. His cheeks were freshly shaven, and his eyes bright and alert, as if he had enjoyed a full eight hours of untroubled slumber.

He caught her glance; his eyes laughed down into her own, and he taunted her softly, 'Sleep well?'

Kit's breath hissed through her teeth, and the dark liquid swayed violently in the cup as if rocked by a sudden storm.

Men! she thought bitterly. It was all a joke to them. Well, Brook would find that she could laugh too. At herself, and at him. Drawing on every ounce of her reserves, she stretched her lips into an answering grin that bared her tiny teeth, and more nearly resembled a snarl as she lied sturdily, 'Like a log. How about you?'

His eyes narrowed, registering her shot, but before he had time to return it Jesse suggested, 'When we've all recovered enough, why don't we go on a tourist trip of the island? No, I don't mean an organised thing,' as Lois made a motion of protest. 'Just the four of us. I can borrow a four-wheel-drive vehicle from our base in town. I thought Kit might like to see something of the forests while she is here.'

'He can't keep away from his beloved trees for long, even when he's supposed to be on holiday,' Lois teased, and her husband grinned good-naturedly.

'True, but they're another aspect of the islands for Kit to experience.'

'You mustn't let her get near to the manchineel trees, Jesse,' Lois warned her husband, looking suddenly worried. 'They're an experience of the islands she can well do without.'

There was more than one experience of the islands she could have done without, Kit thought with a vitriolic glance in Brook's direction, but out loud she said, with a commendable lack of emphasis, 'What's so wrong with manchineel trees?'

She was not overly interested in trees, but it gave her an excuse to turn away from Brook, and at least appear to ignore his mocking look which felt as if it was boring a hole between her shoulder-blades.

'They're deadly. Even water dripping off the leaves after a rainstorm will bring you out in blisters if it falls on you,' Lois answered, and Jesse confirmed gravely,

'The fruit is highly toxic, too. One bite, and . . .' His dismissive gesture told graphically what might be the outcome, but he added comfortingly, 'Don't worry. All the manchineel trees in the forest have been identified, and the barks are marked with a splash of red paint to warn people not to go anywhere near them. The ones nearest to the public paths have big notices tacked on them as well.'

Brook ought to wear a splash of red paint, and a notice, warning people in large letters, 'Danger! Keep your distance!' Would she have heeded it last night, Kit wondered, if he had?

She tried in vain to keep distance between them when Jesse returned later with a four-wheel-drive runabout, and invited them cheerfully to, 'Hop aboard!' The runabout was designed to hold four people, and equipment. The back seat was a bench style, with lockers underneath, and a polished surface. To Kit's dismay, Jesse helped Lois into the front seat beside himself.

'It's best for you girls not to sit together on this trip,' he explained. 'The ride might be bumpy, and you'll need a cushion to bounce on,' he teased Kit.

She sent Brook a sidelong glance. He would make a hard cushion. There was not a surplus ounce of flesh on his athletic frame. Last night, she would have leaned against it, and not noticed the hardness. This morning, she shrank from any physical contact with him.

The state of the track took no account of her wishes, however. Little more than a mile from where they started out, a minor landslide blocked their way, the result of heavy rain in the hills the night before. Jesse braked to a halt to survey the pile of mud and stones across the track, and Lois exclaimed, 'What a shame! Now Kit won't get to see the forest.'

'There's another track over to the left that should take us round it.' Jesse was not to be deterred. 'It will be narrower than this track, and a lot rougher, but if Kit doesn't mind a rocky ride . . . ?'

He threw his guest an enquiring glance, and she could do nothing but grit her teeth, and respond with outward cheerfulness, 'Go ahead, I don't mind.'

She hoped fervently that the new track would not prove to be too long, or too rough, and force her to press Brook into service to counter the bumps as Jesse had suggested, and silently she echoed Lois's indignant, 'Do you call *this* a track?' as their driver plunged his vehicle through the trees, on to a barely discernible ribbon of rough stones and tree roots, but her concern was different from that of her hostess.

'It won't be for long,' Jesse assured them. 'Hold tight!'

There was nowhere for Kit to hold on to, except Brook. The front passenger-seat boasted a grab-rail, but, denied such a convenient anchor herself, Kit dug her toes desperately into the floor to prevent herself from sliding towards Brook, as the vehicle tilted sideways on a hazardous camber.

Momentarily her toe-hold acted as a brake, and then the wheels jolted against a sizeable tree root, and shook her from her precarious hold, and she glissaded rapidly towards Brook's side of the vehicle, with the inevitability of a steel towards a magnet.

He grinned, and opened his arms wide to catch her. 'The Caribbean version of a seatbelt,' he laughed, and his fingers locked together on her other side with such smooth efficiency that Kit almost imagined she could hear them go 'clunk click'.

She was trapped, and the magnetism was just as strong as it had been the night before, and today she had drunk no rum to shield her from its full effects. It sliced through her like a sword, impaling her beleaguered senses, and fear shuddered in its wake.

How much longer would she have the strength to resist its pull? she wondered apprehensively. Her worst enemy was her own femininity, which responded to the male messages flowing from Brook with a waywardness that she found almost impossible to control. In her state of heightened awareness, the manchineel tree came upon her like a warning.

'Stay in your seats, and look at it from a safe distance,' Jesse advised them as he drew to a halt near to the first trunk they came across which bore the scarlet warning splash. 'This is close enough. The leaves may still be dripping from last night's rain, and we're well clear of the canopy here.'

Kit eyed the tree soberly. Except for the tell-tale warning banner, it might have been just any tree. The canopy was thick, inviting rest beneath its shade. The fruit beckoned, tempting hands to pick. Just as Brook was a man like other men, but now, on closer acquaintance, she had learned the difference, and the danger, but it was not so simple to stay clear of Brook.

'Remember what happened to Eve when she picked the apple,' he murmured in Kit's ear, and she turned startled eyes to rake his face. His look held amusement, and derision, and something else which she could not define, but which locked into her stare with a force that rendered her powerless to pull away.

She thought bemusedly, He doesn't really mean Eve and the apple. He means himself, and me. Brook was well aware of his own attraction, and the gleam in his eyes challenged her, daring her to reach out and pick the fruit, and risk the consequences.

Was it possible that the magnetism worked both ways? The thought left her shaken. Her eyes searched Brook's face for an answer, but his expression gave nothing away, and she hated him for guarding his own secret, while reading hers all too clearly. The choice was her own, and it was clear that he was determined to offer her no help. Take it, or leave it, was the message which came across. It was a matter of indifference to him, either way.

It would be a matter of life or death to her. Kit felt a depressing affinity with Eve, who had picked and tasted and suffered, as all women had suffered ever since, she thought bitterly, while the men escaped unscathed, untroubled by prior doubt, or subsequent regret.

It seemed like a lifetime before Jesse set the vehicle rolling again, and they regained the main track above the landslide where, for all its comparative smoothness, Brook continued to weld her palpitatingly close to him, mocking her wriggles of protest with a virtuous, 'Jesse told me to cushion the bumps for you.'

'He didn't mean forever.'

The feel of Brook's arms round her was raising bumps of a different sort on Kit's every tingling nerve-end, but contrarily she did not want them to set her free when Jesse pulled up in a clearing at one side of which was an obviously new plantation of trees, and released his passengers with, 'It's quite safe for you to walk about here, if you want to. There aren't any trees or shrubs that are likely to harm you.'

He lifted Lois down, and left Brook to perform the same service for Kit, and she felt lost, and helpless, and very far from safe when he held her deliberately suspended for a tantalising moment, with her face on a level with his own. His grey eyes seemed to pierce right into the deepest recesses of her mind, and she could not meet his look.

'Put me down. *Please*,' she hissed urgently, and he lowered her unhurriedly to stand beside him, but when her feet were safely on the ground his arm round her shoulders prevented her from moving away from him.

'The ground's slippery after the rain,' he remarked unarguably, since Jesse kept his arm about his wife to steady Lois for the same reason.

'Show Kit the Lazy Mary, Brook,' Jesse called over his shoulder as he bent to check on one of the labelled saplings, and unwittingly foiled her bid to remain beside himself and Lois.

'Go on, touch the leaves,' Brook urged Kit as he drew her apart from the others to the far side of the clearing, beside a tree that bore delicate ferny foliage.

'What will happen if I do?' Kit eyed Brook suspiciously.

'You won't know until you try it.'

He was forcing her to experience everything for herself, just as he had done from the start, refusing to warn her what might be in store, and demanding that she trust him, while giving her absolutely no reason to do anything of the kind.

Kit's lips tightened as he mocked her hesitation, 'Scared?'

'Of course not,' she lied, and forced her shrinking fingers towards the leaves. 'Oh!' The moment she touched them, they recoiled, and Kit turned on Brook indignantly. 'You might have warned me.'

'If I had, the effect wouldn't have had the same impact. You will always remember that Lazy Mary now.'

It was as nothing to the impact Brook was having upon her, and every moment of the time she had spent with him would be etched on her memory forever, Kit thought raggedly, no matter what else she might forget.

'That tree is a magnificent specimen of its kind,' Jesse admired as he strolled over with Lois to join them, and identified the surrounding forest giants for Kit's benefit. 'That one over there, Kit, has a habit of growing on the spot where another tree has fallen down.'

Kit stared fixedly at the tree to which he pointed. First, the poison tree. And now, this one, a new life from the broken remains of an old one. The forest seemed to be trying to tell her something, but what?

Without thinking, her hands raised in a small, appealing gesture towards the massive trunk, as if begging it for an answer, but it was

Brook's voice which reached her ears, and Brook's hand which held her back as Jesse and Lois strolled on. He asked, perceptively, 'What is it you're looking for, Kit?'

His narrowed, searching eyes said that his question was not about trees, nor about things to paint, but about herself, and Kit went pale as he swung her to face him, waiting for her to answer. His forefinger under her chin tilted her face towards him, forcing her to look up at him, and her eyes were a tormented mixture of conflicting emotions as he demanded, 'What is it, Kit?'

How could she tell him what it was, when she scarcely knew herself what it was she was seeking, or even—her breath came unevenly—or even if she had found it, without looking? Her mind answered, Peace, while her heart cried, You! and, not daring to voice either, she took refuge in flippancy.

'Just checking proportions for a possible painting later on.' She sketched an exaggerated gesture, as of a learner artist checking on detail which her own trained eye could judge instinctively, and out of its corner she watched Brook's jaw tighten.

He recognised her answer for what it was, and his look warned her that she could not continue to evade him, that later he would force a reckoning, but it did not prevent Brook from taking numerous photographs for her afterwards, when a flight of scarlet ibis rose from a nearby swamp in a fiery splash of colour. The birds circled the trees, and Kit mourned, 'If only I'd got my sketch-block. I'll never have another opportunity like this.'

'I'll photograph them for you. It will capture the shapes, and the colours, and you can use them to work up a picture with later.'

He was generous with his film. He focused and snapped repeatedly as the flight broke formation, and reformed again and again, until at last the birds began to sink back among the trees, seeking the fiddler crabs to be found in the swamp below. A sigh escaped Kit.

'I wouldn't have missed that for the world,' she breathed ecstatically.

'Neither would I,' Brook answered quietly, and his eyes rested on Kit's face and not on the sky, but she was too absorbed in watching the last stragglers of the flock to notice.

The small episode formed a truce between them, and Kit enjoyed to the full the colourful markets when Jesse drove them down from the hills, and through a series of sizeable villages along the rugged coastline, to where a produce and craft market was in full swing.

Coming from the well-stocked yacht, they had no need of produce, but the crafts drew them.

'Whoever fashioned this from solid wood must be a master craftsman!' Kit exclaimed admiringly, tracing a wondering forefinger across the intricately carved wing of a life-sized humming-bird feeding from a hibiscus flower.

'Take it back with you as a souvenir,' Brook suggested, but Kit shook her head.

'I can't, I——'

'I'll buy it for you, if you're running short of currency.' He misunderstood her hesitation.

'It isn't that, it's just too heavy. I stacked so much painting material into my luggage, if I'm not careful I shall be over the baggage allowance, and I can't jettison my work. After all, it's what I came here to do. I'll take one of these little spice baskets instead,' she decided, turning away from the wood carving. 'The basket will hardly weigh anything.' She sniffed at the tangy mixture of nutmeg and cinnamon, and others to which she could not put a name, and explained, 'I want a present for a friend of mine. She'll love this.'

'She?'

Was it her imagination that Brook's tone sharpened? Kit glanced up at him in surprise, and explained, 'Maggie.'

'Who's Maggie?' His voice was lazily
curious, and she satisfied it with,

'Maggie is my next-flat neighbour, and a very
good friend.' With reservations, she told him
about Maggie, carefully leaving out the reason
why she had been such a good friend.

'But that means you won't have a souvenir
of the islands for yourself.'

Kit shrugged. 'I'll have a copy of your uncle's book when it's published. It will carry a
selection of my paintings and sketches. Those
will have to do. After all, I'm not here on
holiday.'

'But you must have something special, for
yourself. I insist,' he said as Kit made a move
of protest. 'I'll give you something to remember the islands by.'

'Perhaps another spice basket, then,' Kit
began tentatively, but Brook passed on beyond
the spices and the wood carvings to a stall
which offered classic jewellery, all of it hand-
crafted, and with prices to match.

He picked out something which dangled
from a thin gold chain, and the stall-holder remarked, 'The lady will like that. It's made of
black coral.'

Kit's eyes widened. 'Black coral? Oh, Brook,
no; I couldn't possibly accept anything so
costly.'

'It weighs even less than the spice basket.'

'That's not the point. You can't compare the two. The spice basket only cost me coppers, whereas that...'

'The only comparison that matters is that one is to smell, and the other is to wear.' Brook brushed aside Kit's concern. 'The question is, do you like it? If you don't I'll put it back, and choose something else for you.'

He swung it gently at face level, like a tiny pendulum, the better for her to see, and Kit's eyes fixed on the small hanging pendant.

'It's a dolphin,' she discovered, 'just like the ones on your cuff-links.'

'You could say he's a link between us, then, couldn't you?' Brook quipped, but the levity on his lips failed to reach his eyes, which held a keenly searching look as they rested on Kit's face while he waited for her to tell him whether or not she liked his choice.

Kit hesitated. Brook's choice of words struck a note of caution in her. She did not know whether she wanted a link with him or not. If she accepted the pendant, it would act as a permanent reminder of him. Was that wise?

Had he chosen that particular pendant, out of all the others on offer, because he thought she would like it? Or had he deliberately chosen the dolphin in order to underline his own power, as head of the international shipping fleet which bore its name? To emphasise to her that he was acting as her escort, merely as a favour to his uncle, and not in any degree to help herself?

'Don't you like it?' The pendant swung warningly back towards its place on the stall, and the movement wrenched from Kit a gasped admission,

'Yes, oh, yes, I do. I love it.'

How could she not? The skilled fingers of the carver had caught the arched back in joyous mid-leap. The tiny, sensitively worked face seemed to laugh at her, urging her to join in its play, and Kit capitulated with a helpless, 'I think he's absolutely sweet.'

An answering smile parted her lips, betraying her enslavement, and Brook said crisply, 'That settles it, then. He's yours. Stand still, while I fasten him on you.'

He reached round her neck to join the delicate chain together, and although Kit's feet remained obediently rooted to the spot an uncontrollable shiver shook her as she felt Brook's hands touch her skin. It was as if, by choosing the dolphin, he was fixing his seal upon her.

He felt the shiver, and paused, and looked down at her in silence for what seemed a long moment, and, desperate to fill the void, Kit faltered, 'I—I don't know how to thank you. It's a lovely souvenir. Much nicer than I would have chosen for myself.'

'You can thank me properly later on.' Brook's eyes held the glint of promise, and as she saw it a hot flush rose to stain Kit's throat and cheeks.

He paid the stall-holder, and the eyes of the two men met in shared amusement above Kit's head, when she exclaimed, 'No, please, Brook, I want to wear it!' when the man offered her a box in which to carry her gift if she wanted to take it off again.

The small pendant seemed to act like a charm on the rest of the day. The hours sped happily for Kit, with all hint of tension between herself and Brook vanished as if it had never been.

She stood beside him, awed into silence by a thunderous waterfall, but sheltered from its spray by the voluminous plastic sheet which Jesse had sorted out from among the equipment stored inside their box seat.

'There are only two of these sheets, but they're big enough to shelter us all,' her host said, handing one of them over to Brook, and draping the other over himself and Lois.

Brook laughed down at Kit as he tucked the other sheet round her and himself, enclosing them both within its folds. 'You'll be safe from the spray under this.'

Safe enough from the spray, but not safe from the myriad sensations which engulfed her as he drew the plastic round them, enclosing them in a small, intimate tepee of their own. Nervously, Kit's hand flew upwards in the old, unconscious gesture, but instead of tucking a strand of hair behind her ear, as had been her wont, her fingers fled instead to clasp the tiny dolphin for reassurance.

Brook's downward glance latched alertly on to the change, and his smile broadened, as if he was satisfied about something, but Kit was too busily engaged in watching where she trod on the spray-wet and slippery ground to notice as he led her to a vantage-point from which to view the waterfall.

'It's a spectacular sight, isn't it?'

Kit nodded dumbly. The water hurled itself over the abyss with a reckless abandon, and disappeared into some infinite depths below them, out of sight, and, watching it, Kit sensed that she herself was poised on just such an abyss, and that her feet were already beginning to slip helplessly towards its edge.

Jesse chose a smoother road for their return journey, enabling Kit to remain in her seat un-assisted, and contrarily she felt bereft. She glanced across the expanse of seat between herself and Brook, and his return look read her lack, and teased her, and her hand flew up again to clasp the miniature dolphin, which seemed to throb with a borrowed life from the wild, erratic beat of the pulse at the base of her throat against which the tiny pendant rested.

Was this what Maggie meant? What the ancient forest tree had tried to tell her? Kit wondered disjointedly. That in spite of her experience with Paul she must grasp at happiness if it ever came her way again?

What had Brook meant when he had said she could thank him properly later on? In spite of her bravado last night, would she have the courage to grasp at that kind of happiness, if it was offered?

Would it be offered, or not?

Kit's fingers tightened round her pendant, and then held on to it tighter still, as if clinging to a lifeline, when Jesse drew up finally at the jetty from which they had set out that morning, and decanted them from their borrowed transport to take the rowing boat back to the yacht. The official in charge of the small harbour ejected from the door of his office when they came into sight, as if he had been awaiting their return, and he called out, 'Mr

Joyner-Galloway? I've got a message here for you, about a consignment of coconut fibre. The plantation manager asked me to give it to you. Sign here for it, will you, Mr Joyner-Galloway?'

'Just Galloway. The Joyner no longer applies,' Brook answered him quietly, and signed for the printed sheet, which he scanned quickly and then commented, 'That's much better than I expected. The consignment will be ready the day after tomorrow. It will give us one more day of sightseeing, and then...'

Kit scarcely heard him. She stood as if frozen, and watched with a feeling of despair as the fragile bubble of her newly found happiness shattered in front of her eyes.

Joyner-Galloway. Not Manning, as she had supposed. And now just plain Galloway, because the Joyner no longer applied. She felt a hysterical desire to laugh, and an equally urgent need to weep. Joyner was no longer joined.

She already knew that. She had read about it in one of the national newspapers, which had given a short account of Fleur Joyner-Galloway's husband divorcing his wife on the grounds of adultery. The divorce had not been contested. A gasp of pure anguish escaped Kit, and she swayed on her feet.

What cruel twist of fate had made her fall in love with the ex-husband of the woman who had stolen Paul from her?

# CHAPTER SEVEN

WHEN they returned to the yacht, Kit's ashen face gave her the only excuse she needed to escape to her cabin.

Lois cried concernedly, 'Oh, you poor dear, we've tired you out. We're so used to the heat ourselves, we forget how wearing it can be for other people.'

Jesse offered generously, 'You needn't come on the raft trip tomorrow, if you don't feel up to it, Kit.'

The excursion had been mentioned as a fitting end to her stay on the islands, and Kit grasped at it now as if it were indeed a life raft.

'But I want to. I've enjoyed every minute of today, truly I have. I shall be fine by tomorrow. A night's rest is all I need to put me right.'

If her heart was to survive this second blow, she would urgently need occupation to stop herself from thinking, and the prospect of a day spent resting on the yacht in Brook's company, if Lois and Jesse were to go on the raft trip by themselves, panicked her.

If only she had known who Brook was, right from the start. If only the habit of first names at first sight had not led her into assuming that his surname must be the same as that of his uncle. If only...

The 'if only's of this world caused most of its trouble, Kit reflected wearily as she tossed through yet another sleepless night, staring into the darkness through swimming eyes. What a fool Fleur had been, to prefer Paul to her own husband! What even greater folly that she herself had fallen in love with Brook. She had not wanted to. She had believed that it was impossible for her to love again, after Paul. But it had happened, and this love was different, more mature, and correspondingly more painful.

At the time of the inquest Kit had felt grateful that Fleur's husband had not appeared. Illogically, she had felt the guilt which Paul had not, and later there had been no accompanying Press photograph to the announcement of the Joyner-Galloway divorce, so the betrayed husband had remained, for Kit, a shadowy, unrecognised figure, someone in the background.

Through her own distress, she had felt for the unknown man. However harrowing her own parting from Paul, it had been instant, and final, with no time for recriminations, whereas divorce, with all its acrimony, dragged on.

Fleur's husband had lost no time in ridding himself of his unfaithful wife, aided, no doubt, by the fact that there were no children to complicate the settlement. Maggie had read the newspaper report with avid interest, and relayed the details with relish to Kit.

'He's let her have the house and all its contents. It sounds as if he doesn't want any souvenirs of the marriage.'

'He must be the unforgiving type,' Kit had answered indifferently. 'Those sort don't try to build bridges. But I suppose if you're rich enough, and ruthless enough, cutting knots is easy.' She had shrugged away the thing that was no longer her concern.

'Would you have tried to build bridges, in his shoes?' Maggie had countered gently. 'If Paul had lived, would you have gone back to him? Or would you have done what Fleur's husband has done, and divorced him?'

Would she? The question gave Kit pause now. If Paul had escaped from the accident unscathed, the likelihood was that she would have divorced him. But if he had lived, and been disabled by his injuries, would she have been tough enough to cut him adrift?

There could be no satisfactory answer to a
question that was hypothetical anyway. Kit
turned on her side and closed her smarting eyes
to try to blot it out, and woke to find the yacht
under way.

'You're awake at last.' Lois popped her head
round Kit's cabin door, and she sat up and
peered through the porthole.

'We're at sea,' she discovered with surprise.

'We put off hours ago, but I wouldn't wake
you up. You looked shattered last night. Brook
raised the sails so the noise of the engine
wouldn't disturb you. He and Jesse have been
taking turn about at the wheel.'

Kit's heart misgave her. She was discovering
too late that Brook could be kind, as well as
dictatorial. She answered in a muffled voice,
'So you've decided not to go on the raft trip,
after all?'

'No, of course not. It's a great experience,
and if you feel up to it it would be a shame for
you to miss it. But it's on a different island.
We'll be docking soon, so I'll go and get you
some breakfast while you get dressed.'

Another day, another island. Something new
to see and experience, to keep her mind from
thinking. Practice makes perfect, Kit told
herself bitterly as she showered away the signs

of her overnight distress, and steeled herself to face the day ahead.

A day in which she must walk and talk with Brook as if nothing had happened, no secret of his had been uncovered that split her world apart. Not for the first time, Kit blessed the happy chance that had made her insist upon working under her maiden name. In preserving her anonymity, she could keep the secret of her own past, while she came to terms with that of Brook.

When she had washed and dressed, her eyes fell on the dolphin pendant. It lay where she had dropped it the night before, next to her wristwatch on the dressing-table top, waiting to be worn. Yesterday, when Brook had bought it for her, she had not wanted to take it off. Now she felt as if she did not want ever to wear it again.

'I can't,' she whispered. The delicate chain would surely close about her throat if she tried to put it on. Knowing what she did, she could not bear to look at the tiny, laughing face of the dolphin. It seemed to laugh at her, mocking her despair. The dolphin was Brook's mark, and its joy was not for her to share.

'I can't...'

'Can't what?' Lois enquired cheerfully. She nudged open the door with her knee, and brought in a tray containing croissants and orange juice, and regarded Kit with her head held to one side.

'Your new pendant will just set off that white cotton top,' she said, forgetting her own question in the more immediate interest of dress. 'The black coral will show up beautifully against the broderie.'

There was no escape. She had to wear it, or risk attracting comment, and questions which she was not prepared to answer. Kit's fingers fumbled with the clasp, and trembled so much that they were unable to co-ordinate the two ends, to fasten them together. She stiffened her hands, trying to stop their shaking, and only made her efforts even more ineffectual.

'Let me do it.' Lois noticed her difficulty and mistook the cause, and took the chain from Kit's nerveless grasp. 'You're not properly awake yet, and no wonder after the hectic day we had yesterday. But, I promise you, today will be a lot more peaceful, although you'll find it just as interesting. There.' She closed the clasp and stepped back to admire the effect. 'That looks lovely.'

'These are wonderful.' Kit bit into a croissant she did not want in order to hide her shrinking aversion to wearing the pendant. The dolphin lay heavily against her, burning into her flesh

through the thin cotton top. Brook's mark.
Brook's brand. Surely it would leave a dolphin-
shaped scar where it rested. The pain of it felt
so real that Kit's hand rose to lift the tiny
carving away from her skin, and Lois smiled,
and teased,

'At least having the pendant to hold will give
your hair a rest. Come up on deck when you've
finished. I'll go and get together what I need
for the day.'

What Kit felt she most needed was courage
to face the hours that lay ahead, and this time
there was no Maggie to come to her aid. She
used a second glass of orange juice to wash
down the croissant which she doubted if she
would otherwise be able to swallow, spinning
out the frugal breakfast for as long as possible,
but at last it was finished, and she could find
no further excuse to remain below deck any
longer.

Sounds of berthing floated down a warning
to her: the slap of a rope being thrown ashore,
Jesse's voice calling, 'OK, Brook, I've got her,'
and a gentle bump as a fender touched lightly
against something solid.

It was time to go and join the others. Time
to nerve herself to meet Brook, knowing the
secret of his past, and having somehow to
endure the ordeal of keeping her own, without

him suspecting that there was anything amiss, or different from the shining happiness that had been between them yesterday, and which seemed like a lifetime ago.

The moment Kit appeared on deck, Brook stopped what he was doing, and turned round. Even though she had thought her rope-soled canvas shoes made no sound, his fine-tuned alertness was aware of her presence, and knew in exactly which spot to look for her.

Meeting his gaze, Kit stumbled to a halt, and sounds of the busy harbour beyond the rail faded from her consciousness. Lois's cheerful chatter, and Jesse answering his wife, became an indistinguishable background noise, and there was only a pair of grey eyes, seeming to pierce into the very depths of her mind.

Kit wanted to close her own lids, as a defence against them, and then Brook looked downwards, his glance came to rest on the dolphin pendant, and he smiled. Achingly, Kit loved the small curving of his lips, which gentled the stern lines of his face, and softened the steely grey of his eyes with a warmth which she knew despairingly was intended for her alone, and her heart wept.

It was a torture equivalent to offering poisoned food to the starving. If she took it, she would die from shame, because then Brook must learn of the dreadful thing which lay between them, and he would surely hate her and reject her because of it, even though it had not been her fault.

If she refused the food, as she must, she would condemn herself to remain empty for the rest of her days.

Brook asked softly, 'Are you feeling rested enough to go on the raft trip, Kit? If not...'

Mundane words, which pierced her like a knife because they showed he cared. But he cared only because he did not know. The anguish of her secret stirred Kit into hasty speech.

'I feel fine this morning, thanks.'

Reaching desperately back into the past, for the armour which she had so carelessly abandoned the day before, she pinned on the brittle smile which the world had come to recognise after Paul, and, gaining confidence from its shelter, she repeated more firmly, 'I can't wait to find out what it's like to ride on a raft. I'm looking forward to it.'

That at least was true. She could not wait to grasp at any activity which would prevent her from thinking, and there was nothing else, either now or in the future, for her to look forward to.

Jesse called out from the harbour walkway, 'I've made her fast,' and Brook turned to answer him, and the spell was broken. Released from the need to armour herself against Brook's smile, Kit felt suddenly sick and faint. Her limbs resembled jelly, like a puppet whose strings had been suddenly cut through, leaving her knees in danger of buckling, and dropping her unceremoniously on the deck.

Lois knotted the strings together again with a firm, 'If you don't feel up to coming on the raft trip you must say so, Kit.'

The eyes of her hostess were keen on her paling face, and Kit noticed confusedly that they took time off to glance in Brook's direction, as if their owner was busily putting two and two together, and finding her sum total to be perilously close to the truth. Kit begged her earnestly, and low, 'I'm fine, Lois, really. Please, don't make a fuss...'

In spite of herself her voice cracked, and she was unable to go on, but the urgent appeal in her eyes spoke for her, and with quick perception Lois took the message on board. She answered gently, and equally quietly, so that her words would not reach the ears of the two men, 'I won't, I promise. But if you want a shoulder to cry on mine has had plenty of practice with the schoolchildren.'

Maggie's opposite number, half a world away! The kindly offer was nearly Kit's undoing, and, reading the struggle for control on her suddenly working face, Lois raised her voice and quickly stemmed the threatening flood with a schoolteacher-like briskness which she must have used countless times in the classroom, and which had the desired effect now.

'Right, have you all got everything you need for the day before we go?'

'Just hark at Chalkie,' Jesse teased, and Kit joined in the general laughter, along with Lois herself, and glanced her gratitude at her hostess as the latter's fingers closed briefly but encouragingly over her own, suspecting the cause of her distress, but thankfully not knowing its full extent.

Nobody could, except for herself, and the need to keep it that way made Kit's laughter more brittle, and her voice just a shade higher than usual as they boarded the raft that was to carry them on their eight-mile journey.

Kit carefully kept her face averted as Brook reached out a hand to help her on to the platform of skilfully lashed bamboo poles that made up the raft, but the grip of his hand on her arm, meant to steady her, had the opposite effect, and, feeling her stiffen, he said reassuringly, 'There's no need for you to feel nervous. These rafts are more solid than they look. They're built to carry cargo. You won't weigh half so much as one of those.' He gestured to a stack of crates already on board, and containing cans of soft drinks.

'Yes. I mean, no. I'm not really nervous,' Kit stammered.

Brook's closeness, the deep, gentle timbre of his voice, aimed to steady her, rocked her self-control more than the bobbing raft, and her own voice betrayed her lie, and, mistaking the cause of its wobble, Brook turned and opened his arms wide, and invited her with a laugh, 'Clip on a Caribbean seatbelt?'

Kit shrank back. 'No, Brook. No!' As he looked as if he might clasp her to him willy-nilly, she cried, 'I...'

She gave a hunted look round her, seeking Lois, and saw to her dismay that the other couple were already stepping on to a second raft, becoming a part of its cargo, which was similarly stacked to their own.

'I thought we'd be riding together,' she began urgently, and the rafter smiled.

'If we split up the party it evens the load, and gives us both a fare.'

In the face of such generosity, what could she do but accept the inevitable? Kit sank down reluctantly beside Brook as the rafter, pole in hand, his bare feet giving him a firm grip on the rounded bamboo, which shoes would have denied to him, pushed off from the bank into the strongly flowing current, effectively isolating her with Brook.

Now she knew what it was like to be marooned on a desert island, Kit thought without humour, and flinched when Brook demanded, with a frown that drew his dark brows together, 'Why not? What's wrong with a Caribbean seatbelt?'

The rafter provided Kit with a ready-made excuse. She nodded in the man's direction, and whispered urgently, 'Not here. Not now. It's too—too public.'

'You didn't seem to mind the public yesterday.'

Yesterday, she had not known. 'Yesterday was carnival,' she excused herself lamely, and wondered with growing despair from where she would find the strength to hold herself apart from Brook, when her whole body yearned to melt into his arms, and her lips ached for the feel of his kisses.

Kit had only a confused impression of the river journey which followed, of the rafter, poling his craft with consummate skill over deep waters, across shallows, and around bends which spun the raft almost as dizzily as her own turbulent thoughts.

Beside her, she was nervously aware of Brook watching her, unconvinced by her excuses. He folded his arms about his knees, closing their recent invitation, and shutting her out. She blinked back stinging tears, which blurred the identity of several large birds, flying ponderously beside the waterway——at the end of the trip Lois asked her, 'Did you see the herons, Kit?' and Kit thought dully, So that's what they were.

They were to stop for lunch at the aptly named Rafters' Rest, a sophisticated complex catering for the needs of tourists, even to the obligatory swimming-pool, and which made the wild journey they had just undertaken seem a thousand miles away.

The growing conviction that she must make a much longer journey, back home, and that with all possible speed, bore in on Kit like a leaden weight. For the sake of her own sanity, she must get as far away from Brook as it was possible to go, before she was tempted to fling herself into his arms, and blurt out her ghastly secret, and then her heart would die within her when those same arms pushed her away from him in disgust.

She ducked under one of them when Brook tried to throw it across her shoulders, and draw her to him as they stepped ashore from the raft, but she was not quite quick enough to avoid his flashing hand. His angry fingers grasped her round the wrist, and spun her to face him.

'I ought to re-christen you Mary,' he growled.

The unexpectedness of it stilled Kit's struggle to be free. 'Why...?'

'Because every time I get near to you you back off quicker than the leaves of the Lazy Mary.' His voice gravelled out the words, accusing her. 'You've changed since yesterday. Why? What's happened?'

Kit swallowed hard and forced out, 'Nothing's happened. How could it? You were with me all day.'

'Something has, and I mean to find out what. I——'

'Oh, Kit, do come and have a look at these model rafts. They're just perfect.' Lois broke through the threatening storm, and Kit grabbed at the opportunity to twist away from Brook's hold, and ran over to where Lois was examining a display at the counter of the souvenir shop.

'I must have one of these, Jesse!' his wife exclaimed.

'You shall have one each——' Jesse agreed generously, but Brook cut in with,

'I'll buy Kit's. As a reminder,' he added significantly, and his steely glance told her that his gift was to make sure she did not forget his threat to find out what had happened to change her attitude, and not merely as a souvenir of the raft trip.

He put the small-scale model into her hands, and Kit looked down at it frozenly. A life raft, which, if she stepped on to it, would bring her nothing but further pain and suffering, and, if she did not, she would drown. Darker shadows than they had ever known clouded Kit's eyes as she raised them reluctantly to Brook's face, struggling against a closed throat to force through suitable words of thanks, but Brook spoke first, and his voice sounded oddly hoarse.

'Kit . . . Kit, I——'

'Hi, Brook! This is a happy chance, meeting you here. I need to see you about another consignment of fibre. Can you find me enough hold space, quickly, to take a second load?'

Brook swore, briefly and forcefully, under his breath, but only the rigidity of his jaw betrayed his feelings as he turned to face the newcomer.

'Hello, Mike. Yes, we've got a vessel due to dock tomorrow, about noon. She'll be unloading, so she should be able to take your second load of fibre on the turn-around.'

'That's great. Sorry to have interrupted your party.' The man smiled at Kit, innocent of the crackling tension around him.

Equally unaware, Jesse invited, 'Why not join us for lunch, Mike? You and Brook could talk shop while we eat, unless it's anything too confidential. This is the finish of the holiday for us, so you won't be spoiling anything by talking about work.'

'It sounds a great idea. It'll save me a mint of time,' Mike beamed, and Kit could have jumped for joy. The newcomer's presence during the meal would save the conversation from becoming personal.

He proved to be chatty and expansive, and in the more relaxed atmosphere Kit was able to swallow sufficient food to prevent comment upon her lack of appetite, and she could hardly contain her eagerness when he suggested to Brook as they reached the coffee stage, 'You say your holiday's over, so why don't we go to the office now, and get the paperwork settled?

That way, we might be able to get the two consignments of fibre shipped together.'

'I didn't say—Jesse did. As a matter of fact, I——' Brook began, when Jesse intervened.

'You go ahead, Brook. I'll take Lois and Kit home on the islander, and you can sail the *Dolphin* back and join us there when you're through.'

'I can't do that.' Brook's expression registered his frustration. 'All your gear is on the *Dolphin*. The girls' clothes...'

'There's nothing you can't do without for a couple of days, is there, ladies?' Jesse turned to his wife and Kit, and they both chorused,

'No, nothing at all.'

'That's settled, then,' Jesse beamed, and demolished any further objection by Brook with an unarguable, 'It will be another new experience for Kit, to see the islands from the air.'

Amid the general goodbyes, it was comparatively easy for Kit to avoid being alone with Brook. She attached herself to Lois's side with the determination of a limpet, lowering her lids to avoid the frustrated anger in Brook's glare when, on the pretext of planting a light kiss on her forehead, a replica of his salutation to Lois, he gritted in her ear, 'We'll talk the moment I get back.'

If the others had heard him, they would probably have taken it to mean that they would talk about his uncle's book, but his threat was enough to warn Kit that when the *Dolphin* sailed back into the harbour fronting Jesse's house she must be long gone.

Her eyes blurred as she gazed downwards from the plane window an hour later, and picked out the familiar dolphin pennant fluttering from the masthead of the large white yacht, whose creamy wake told her that it was moving fast, under engine power, as if the man at the helm was anxious to get his business finished as quickly as possible.

The figure at the wheel raised an arm as the plane sped overhead, and instinctively Kit raised her own hand to wave back, even though she knew that it was unlikely Brook would be able to see her through the small window, but it was the only way left to her to send him a silent goodbye.

The plane banked in a turn, following the coastline back along the string of islands, leaving the yacht behind bearing Brook and his business colleague, and, unbeknown to either of them, a small, weeping stowaway that was her heart.

# CHAPTER EIGHT

'BROOK should be back in a couple of days,' Jesse said.

Kit's mind clicked into action. Two days, in which she must manufacture a convincing excuse to give to Lois and Jesse, to explain her hurried departure, book a seat on the first available European flight, and escape before the master of the *Dolphin* returned.

'I've done all I possibly can, here on the islands.' Kit lost no time in pleading her cause the moment the plane landed them on their home airstrip, and reunited Jesse with his own small cutter.

'This is coming down to earth with a vengeance after the *Dolphin*,' he grinned as he headed his craft out of the busy harbour, following the familiar coastline back to its own idyllic anchor.

'We can't expect to live the high life all the time,' Lois answered philosophically. 'Come to that, neither can Brook. He's at work already. The *Dolphin*'s a floating office to him, not just a plaything. Talking of offices, I've got a pile of books waiting to be marked before school starts on Monday,' she grimaced. 'I'll have to get cracking on them first thing to-morrow morning, if I'm going to get them ready for class on time.'

'I must do the same with my sketches.' Kit grabbed at the heaven-sent opportunity to put her case. 'If I'm going to turn them into pub-lishable material in time, I need to get back home fast, and work them up in my studio.'

'Oh, Kit, must you go so soon? Can't you stay with us for just a few more days?'

'Do you absolutely have to go, Kit? We shall miss you tremendously. Brook will be back in a couple of days.'

Only forty-eight hours in which to make her escape. The warning beat like a drum in Kit's mind. The kindly protests of her host and hostess made the prospect of leaving even more difficult, and she had to swallow a lump in her throat before she was able to insist, 'I really must. There's a printing deadline to meet, and I can't shift the goalposts. I'll have to ask you to say goodbye to Brook for me. I'll write and thank him for showing me round the islands when I get home.'

It was cowardice, but it was the best way. The agony of saying goodbye on paper could be borne in private, and if she wrote on her publisher's notepaper, Kit planned, she need not reveal her own home address.

'What about your suitcase of clothes?' Jesse argued. 'It'll still be on board the *Dolphin*, the same as ours.'

'Lois lent me the suitcase, and there aren't many clothes. I took all the necessaries with me on our day out, so there isn't much left in my cabin.' Kit looked across appealingly at Lois. 'Would you do me a favour, and post on to me what there is left?'

'Of course I will. Although I feel more inclined to keep your things here, and make you come back and collect them yourself,' Lois smiled. She leaned across and pressed Kit's hand. 'We've loved having you, and we both want you to promise to come and stay with us again, just as soon as you have some holiday due.'

'That would be lovely,' Kit answered evasively, and her heart twisted. Lois and Jesse had become firm friends during the short time she had been with them, and it hurt to have to cut adrift from them, too, but she dared not run the risk of returning to the islands, and perhaps meeting Brook again.

'In that case I'll tuck your clothes in a drawer, and it will save you from having to pack so much when you come again,' Lois said with satisfaction, but when she came to Kit's room later, to chat while her departing guest packed her case, she asked quietly, 'Wouldn't it be better if you stayed, Kit, to...?' She hesitated, and then went on, 'To finish off things here, before you go home?'

They both knew that she was speaking about Brook, and not about her work, and Kit's hands stilled for a minute as they folded lacy underwear, and then abruptly plunged into the depths of her suitcase to hide their sudden uncontrollable shaking. With her face averted, she answered Lois in a strained voice, 'It wouldn't help. It will be better—much better—if I go home.'

'If you feel you really must.'

Lois made no further demur, except to warn when Kit picked up the telephone to dial the airport, 'They may not have a seat at such short notice.'

Lois voiced Kit's own worst fears, and her fingers clenched on the receiver in a white-knuckled grip as she begged silently, They *must* have a seat. *Please* let them have a seat. She made her needs known to the friendly voice which answered her call, and felt sick with apprehension as she obeyed its request to, 'Just hold on for a moment or two, while I check what is available.'

The wait lasted for a thousand years, and then the voice came back, 'We've got one cancellation. Hello? Hello, are you still there?'

'Yes, I'm still here,' Kit answered faintly, and drew in a deep breath to steady herself sufficiently to answer the request for her name. 'Fielding. Kit Fielding.'

'Your ticket will be ready for you at the desk when you arrive at the airport tomorrow morning, Miss Fielding.'

It was like being invited to pick up her own death warrant. Now the die was cast, and she had obtained the coveted seat, Kit felt as if she was being torn in two. It took every ounce of her strength to retain control the next day, when she said her goodbyes to Lois and Jesse, and wondered dully as the plane took off how it was that her body could continue to survive when its most vital organ was being left so far behind.

Maggie was waiting when Kit arrived home, and the irrepressible Scot was fairly bursting with news. 'Now don't you go flying off anywhere else, at least for the next week or two,' she demanded. 'I want you to be my maid of honour. Or is it bridesmaid now?'

'Bridesmaid,' Kit said firmly, and eyed her friend with a mixture of amusement and disbelief. 'I can't believe you're really going to give up your freedom at last. Is he the same one you were telling me about before I left?'

'The very same. Even I don't change boy-friends that often,' Maggie said indignantly, and held up her erstwhile ringless left hand, which now bore a sparkling diamond. 'Proof, if you don't believe me,' she grinned, and then sobered.

'I said I'd know when the right one came along, Kit, and Robert is special. He thinks the same about me.'

'Nice to be special, to someone.'

There was a depth of wistfulness in Kit's voice that earned her a sharp glance from Maggie, but the latter's tone was brisk as she went on, 'We've both been around for long enough to know our own minds, so there's no need for a long engagement.'

'You said you were going to meet his people, the weekend I left.'

'I did. It was great. We all got on like a house on fire. It wouldn't have made any difference one way or the other, to Robert and me, but it all helps.'

'It sounds perfect. I look forward to meeting him.'

'You'll like one another. His best man is nice, too. And unattached,' Maggie said significantly, and Kit sent her a stern look.

'Stop matchmaking, Maggie; you ought to know by now that I'm a no-go area where that's concerned.'

'Even the Berlin Wall came down eventually,' Maggie retorted, but she obediently changed the subject with, 'Tell me about the Caribbean islands. Did you like the people you stayed with?'

'Lois and Jesse are special, too. They've invited me to go back for a holiday some time.'

'What about Alton Manning's nephew? Wasn't he supposed to be showing you round?'

'He took me with him on his yacht when he visited the islands in the course of his business. He's head of the Dolphin shipping line.'

That made Brook sound suitably old and staid, Kit decided, and hoped it would stem Maggie's curiosity. She did not feel equal to being questioned about Brook. 'We all stayed on his yacht while the carnival was on,' she diverted her friend's attention.

'Wow!' Maggie was suitably impressed. 'Did you get to see all the islands?'

'Most of them. I brought you a present from one of them.' Kit searched out the little spice basket, and watched while Maggie unwrapped her offering.

'It's lovely, Kit.' Maggie sniffed appreciatively. 'Mmmm. Doesn't it smell gorgeous? To think, they actually grow these things out there.'

Released from its wrapping, the small basket wafted warm, pungent spicy aromas across the room, and Kit caught her breath.

In a second, the heady mixture of cinnamon and nutmeg, ginger and mace transported her back among the islands. Back with Brook under waving palm trees, swimming beside him in impossibly turquoise seas, and strolling hand in hand across wave-lapped sands, to borrow the light of the huge tropical moon, while Brook held her in his arms, and enslaved her heart with his kisses. From a long distance away, she heard Maggie enthuse, 'If the islands look half as gorgeous as my spice basket smells, they must be paradise. That break was just what you needed, Kit. You must feel different now you've been away—happier...?'

Different, yes. But happier? Kit took a deep breath and lied valiantly, 'I do. Feel different, I mean.' What she really meant was worse.

'Happier?' Maggie was not to be put off, and Kit nodded vigorously.

'Of course. I'm—I'm—humming-bird happy,' she blurted out, and burst into tears.

She had not cried like this even at Paul's funeral, when she'd buried not only her husband, but everything she had ever believed in. Once she started Kit found she could not stop, and was equally helpless to check her tongue, which poured out her secrets into Maggie's receptive ears. Her words stumbled to a despairing halt with, 'You told me once to love and let go. That's what I've got to do, all over again.'

'You do manage to pick them, don't you?' Maggie remarked drily, and reached for the kettle and the teapot, her panacea for all ills.

'I'm sorry,' Kit gulped. 'I'm making a complete fool of myself.'

'You should have cried it out of your system long ago, instead of working yourself half to death. Work is no substitute for a good howl. Drink this; it'll make you feel better.' Maggie handed over a strong, liberally sugared cup, ignored Kit's grimace of distaste as she obediently sipped the syrupy mixture, and commanded, 'Now go back again to the beginning, and fill in the details for me. I didn't catch half of what you said, you were crying so hard. What's his name, for instance?'

'That was half the trouble. I took it for granted that his surname would be Manning, the same as his uncle. Lois just introduced him as Brook.'

Kit's voice trembled as her tongue lingered over the name, but she carried on bravely, 'He's tall and dark and...'

'...handsome, and Fleur Joyner-Galloway's ex-husband. So what?'

'He's dropped the Joyner bit, since he was divorced. He's just plain Brook Galloway now.'

'The head of the Dolphin shipping line sounds anything but plain to me. What a fool his wife must have been, to throw him over in favour of Paul.'

'That's what I thought,' Kit agreed hollowly, and Maggie gave her a searching look.

'Well, what are you going to do about it?'

'Nothing.'

'You can't just let it rest there, Kit. There's a chemistry between you two, and it won't just go away. It's obviously infected him too; he seems to have made all the running—to start with anyway.'

'He did. I just ran away. At first, that is.'

'You're both free, you both feel the same way, so what's to stop you from...?'

'I can't, Maggie.' Kit's voice rose in a wail. 'If Brook ever found out that Paul was my husband...' Kit's already white face went several shades paler at the prospect.

'It wasn't your fault, for goodness' sake, so he can't possibly blame you. Paul cheated you just as badly as Brook's wife cheated him. If anything, it should give you both something in common...'

Maggie's weak attempt at a joke trailed into silence in the face of Kit's bleak, 'I feel it was mostly Paul's fault. After all, a man makes all the running.'

'You're still living in another world, aren't you?' Maggie looked across at Kit over the rim of her teacup, with a mixture of affection and pity. 'I only saw the woman once, at the inquest, but it was enough to tell me that, whatever was going on between her and Paul, it was just as much her fault as his. She was a Jezebel, if ever I saw one. But that doesn't help to solve your problem now.'

'I'll work it out of my system, I suppose, the same as I did before,' Kit answered flatly, and delighted her publisher a few weeks later with the results of her non-stop grind at her easel, which returned the dark shadows to her eyes, which had known a few fleeting weeks of respite, and put back the hollows in her cheeks that Caribbean cooking had begun to fill out again.

'These are inspired, Kit,' her publisher enthused. 'They're alive. You might have lived every single one of these scenes yourself.'

She had, thanks to Brook. Without interest, Kit heard her companion add, 'These will put your own name in the headlines, as well as that of Alton Manning.'

Kit remained silent. She would have much preferred to forget her name. Far from grasping at fame, she simply wanted to disappear, and take her misery with her, but she was given no choice when her publisher telephoned her the next day.

'Alton Manning's over the moon with what you've done for him, Kit. So much so that he insists you go along with him, to sign copies of his book at the launch. It will be a real feather in our cap to have a top-rank author and a top-rank illustrator on our lists,' he gloated, and destroyed any hope Kit might have had of refusing.

On the day of the launch, Alton Manning called to collect Kit from her home. 'I can make my own way to the bookshop,' she had earlier protested, but the author had insisted,

'You haven't replaced your Metro yet. I heard about the crash. You must still be without wheels.'

He had heard the news from Brook, presumably, Kit had thought dully as the author went on, 'In any case, it will be good for us to be seen to arrive at the launch together. Extra publicity for both of us.'

He was generous in wanting her to share in his own publicity, but Kit's heart contracted. What if, during the journey through London together, he should want to talk about her stay in the Caribbean? How could she bear it, if the talk turned to Brook? Her nerves were strung tight by the time the car arrived to collect her.

'I say,' Maggie breathed in awe, peeping through the curtain of the front window, 'it's a chauffeur-driven limo. You *are* going up in the world, Kit.'

Kit's heart felt as if it was descending in the opposite direction as she ducked through the car door which the chauffeur held open for her, and steeled herself to meet Brook's uncle.

'I've got a surprise for you, young lady,' he greeted her, and panic set in as she realised that there was already someone else with him in the car. A man. If it had not been for the uniformed arm firmly slamming the car door behind her, she would have turned tail and fled. She hardly dared to look at the other passenger. Her heart was a pain in her throat, and blood pounded in her ears, almost shutting out Alton's introduction.

'Carl, here, is head of the consortium which funds the Frame picture galleries. He wants to hold a separate launch in the Midlands at one of his galleries there, and team it with an exhibition of all the paintings you did for me of the Caribbean islands, those which haven't been used in the book, as well as those which have. It seemed a marvellous idea to me. Beneficial to both of us. What do you think, Kit?'

Kit's only recognisable thought was, He's fair-haired. Not black-haired and grey-eyed. Her own eyes clung to the light-coloured hair of the other man in the car, as if it was a lifeline, until she realised dimly that her companions were waiting for her to answer.

'You will come, won't you, Kit?' the author pressed her anxiously, and she managed through a parched throat,

'If—if you really want me to.'

The Midlands. It was not far away, but far enough to provide an escape. Maggie would call it running away. The fair-haired man laughed.

'You're essential. The exhibition will be a solo, for your work alone. Collectors from all over the world come to that particular gallery, and there has already been a good deal of interest shown in your paintings. The book launch, and the paintings that go with it, will be a novel idea, and it should stimulate interest in both.'

'You'll have to learn how to handle fame after this, Kit,' the author teased, and with an effort Kit pinned on her old, defensive smile. Handle fame? It would help her more if she could learn how to handle her own heart.

An exclusive exhibition in a Frame gallery was the ultimate ambition of most artists, and, because of Brook, it meant less than nothing to her, except as a handy distraction from her wretchedness. She should hate him for it, and could not, and her laughter held a hollow ring as she joined in the champagne reception at the bookshop, and then sat down beside Alton at a table stacked high with copies of his book, and was soon busily signing her name under his, to satisfy a queue of eager customers.

The champagne induced a floaty feeling of unreality, and she knew she should have heeded Maggie's warning, 'Eat some breakfast before you go out,' but at least the temporary euphoria dulled the pain.

In the background she could hear Carl chatting to customers, offering them complimentary tickets for the forthcoming exhibition, and Kit voiced her surprise at the eagerness with which they were accepted.

'You're far too modest,' Alton scolded.

'I'm only a commercial artist.'

'You *were* only a commercial artist. These pictures you've done of the Caribbean put your work on an entirely different plane,' Carl disagreed. 'They're inspired. Your work was good before—I've had a number of enquiries about the possibility of purchasing your originals, from collectors. But these paintings have got a new dimension. They're obviously a labour of love.'

Kit flinched as if she had been struck by a lash. How close Carl was to the truth, he would never know. Love was the other dimension, and from now on it would once again be missing from her work, which would make the coming exhibition, and the interest of the collectors, a waste of time. The rest of her life was a waste of time. She wanted to shout the news at Carl, and did not have the courage, and diverted the conversation with a rueful, '"Labour" just about sums it up. I'm glad I'm a painter, and not an author. I've got writer's cramp, after signing all those books.'

It had been a long and exhausting session, and it left Kit with a new respect for clerical workers. Alton consoled, 'Never mind, we'll be able to go soon. It's nearly closing time. I'll take you back home—— Oh, yes, coming,' he broke off as the bookshop manager signalled to him. 'Use the books from this pile,' he told

Kit as he rose from his chair. 'I've already signed them.' And he was gone.

Left by herself, Kit continued to sign doggedly, handing the books to an assistant who hovered near by, ready to wrap the customers' purchases for them.

'Last one,' the girl whispered encouragingly as two hands reached down towards the table, holding a book for Kit to sign. It was ready open, with five fingers spread across the title page, firming it down for her to write.

Long, lean fingers, with fastidiously manicured nails. Tanned fingers, bronzed by the Caribbean sun. Kit's hand froze with her pen poised above the page. The shop lights winked on a glint of gold set in a pristine shirt cuff, neat discs of precious metal engraved with the leaping figure of a dolphin. She remained as if set in stone for what seemed an aeon of time before Brook spoke.

'Kit...' he said.

The curt monosyllable pulled her reluctant eyes upwards to his face. It was set in the stern, unyielding lines she knew so well, and her heart quailed within her.

'I'll wait for you outside.' His tone was equally grim.

There were no other customers waiting whom she could use as an excuse to remain in the shop. The assistant hurried off to close the doors on trade for the day. Alton and Carl had vanished into regions unknown.

'We've got things to say to one another,' the remorseless voice continued.

The knowledge of what she herself could say, and dared not, jolted Kit into speech. She swallowed hard, and stammered, 'Yes. I mean, no...'

'Make up your mind.'

He gave her no quarter. Kit's chin snapped up defensively. 'I'm going back with Alton, in his car.'

'Sign my book first.'

Automatically, Kit signed, because that was what she was here to do. Her hand shook so badly that any self-respecting bank would reject the signature out of hand. Trembling, she closed the volume, and forced herself to hold it out to Brook, and for long moments his fingers gripped its other end, while his eyes held her own in a mesmeric stare, a dual link from which there was no escape.

Kit felt as if she was suffocating. Her head spun, and her senses threatened to desert her, and just as a growing darkness began to gather ominously behind her eyes Brook gave her a curt nod, and turned and walked away.

It was as if an electric current had been switched off between them. Kit's nerveless hands dropped to her sides, and she sank back limply in her chair. She felt as if she had been pulling hard in a tug-of-war, and the opposing team had suddenly let go of the rope, without any warning.

Brook was not a man to accept defeat. What had made him suddenly change his mind? Uneasily Kit went in search of Alton, and found instead the shop manager's secretary.

'Mr Manning said to carry on out to the car, and he'll follow you in a minute or two,' the girl smiled.

Kit's heart thumped uncomfortably as she made her way out of the shop by the staff entrance. A cautious peep along the road confirmed her fears. A sleek silver-grey Jaguar, which could only belong to Brook, was parked some distance away along the street. Through its rear window, she could just make out a figure clad in navy blue, in the driver's seat. He appeared to be deeply engrossed in reading a newspaper.

How like Brook! Temper stiffened Kit's resolve. How like him, to sit calmly reading, assuming that because he had said he would wait for her she would meekly accept his edict, and join him in his car without a murmur of protest.

*That*, for his arrogance! She snapped mental fingers at the distant figure, and hurried across the pavement to where Alton Manning's limousine was parked in front of the shop entrance. The chauffeur saw her coming, and was ready with the door open, and Kit dived inside its sanctuary, and collapsed on to the seat with a sigh of relief. The figure in the Jaguar had neither looked up nor turned round. She was safe.

Kit closed her eyes momentarily as the chauffeur resumed his seat, and the car pulled away from the pavement, only to have her lids fly open again in total disbelief as Brook's voice ordered from the opposite corner of the seat, 'Keep going, Johnson. You know the address.'

Kit stared at him through the gloom as if she was seeing an apparition. 'B-but you said ... I said ... this is Alton's car,' she blurted.

She should have known that Brook would not give in so easily. He was devious, scheming—and eminently successful. He remarked with unruffled calm, 'My chauffeur is waiting to take Alton and Carl out to dinner somewhere.'

My chauffeur. The blue-uniformed figure whom she had mistakenly believed to be Brook himself. He had manipulated his uncle and Carl as successfully as he had tricked herself. He added, 'I told you we had things to talk about.'

He had told her the same thing once before, on a sunny Caribbean afternoon. The memory goaded Kit into a defiant, 'What if I don't want to talk about—things? Whatever they are,' she flung back.

'I intend to find out *why* you don't want to.'

They were back to square one. Silence stretched like a black tunnel between them. Kit stared stolidly out of the window on her side of the car, refusing to look at Brook as the limousine slid smoothly through the evening traffic.

When it stopped outside her flat, she was ready with her hand on the door-handle, and, without waiting for the chauffeur to help her, she flung open the door and jumped out, and fled up the steps, but Brook was right behind her when she put her key in the lock.

On the way up she had seen the curtains twitch at Maggie's window, and she prayed that her next-door neighbour would appear as she usually did, but Maggie must have seen Brook follow her up, and the Scot remained tactfully invisible. With a thumping heart Kit hurried into the tiny hall, walking heedlessly across a small pile of envelopes which lay on her mat.

'You've forgotten these,' Brook said, and picked them up as he followed her inside.

He was so close behind her that she had no opportunity to close the door between them, and one long stride took Brook across the threshold in her wake, without waiting for an invitation.

'You've forgotten these,' he repeated.

They were buff envelopes. Probably statements, or bills. Kit turned dumbly, and held out her hand to take them, and was in time to see Brook's face turn suddenly grey.

He muttered something under his breath, and his eyes were fixed on the see-through window panel of the top envelope. His nostrils dilated on a hard breath. 'No wonder,' he grated, and his glance passed from the envelope to rake Kit's face. Her cheeks paled at the ferocity of his expression, but before she had a chance to speak he went on harshly, '*Mrs Venables*. Paul Venables's wife. The man who was my ex-wife's lover.' His laugh was bitter. 'So this is why you didn't want to talk. You knew, and you deliberately strung me along.' His tone was low, his iron self-control reining in a shout. 'If this is your idea of a joke, it isn't mine,' he snarled.

His face under its tan was bloodless, his lips likewise, a tight white line through which the words spat bullet-like in short, clipped volleys, each one of which found its target in Kit's heart.

'Did you enjoy taking your revenge on me for what my wife did to your marriage?' he gritted.

Only his eyes were outside of his control. They glittered as if with a fever, and the pupils dilated until they turned the cool grey into black that burned like live coals in his ashen face.

The look in them tore speech from Kit's trembling lips. 'The affair couldn't have been all on Paul's side. It takes two to tango. And you lost no time in getting rid of your wife.' Incredibly she heard herself defending Paul, defending the indefensible.

Brook glared. 'Wouldn't you have divorced your husband, if he had survived his accident?' he flung at her, and the brutality of it made Kit gasp.

Maggie had asked her the same thing, but gently, striving to heal the memories. The same question, coming from Brook, struck her like a hammer-blow, and she shrank from the pain of it.

'Would you? Answer me.' Brook's hands were on her shoulders, shaking her, his eyes boring down into her face, and burning into her mind. 'Would you?'

'I . . . I . . .'

'Think about it, *Mrs Venables*,' he sneered. 'Before you condemn me for cutting myself free from Fleur, ask yourself if you wouldn't have done the same, given the chance. But you didn't get the chance, did you? Instead, you took out your revenge on me. I hope you enjoyed it.'

Ignoring Kit's gasp of protest, he flung the incriminating envelopes down on to the hall table, and, with one backward look that seemed to spear right through her, spun on his heel and strode to the door.

In a daze of shock Kit heard it slam behind him, and the sound of his footsteps running down the stairs. One buff envelope, and then the others, slid off the polished table-top and fluttered to the floor with a sigh, but Kit ignored them. They had done all the damage it was possible for them to do.

The sound of the limousine starting away from the kerb stirred her from her trance. She swayed on her feet, and sank dizzily on to a nearby chair, her knees buckling as her face crumpled, and, for the second time, tears got the upper hand.

Kit could not remember clearly how she spent the next twenty-four hours. Maggie came and went, promising, 'I'll pop in the moment I get back from work,' so when the doorbell rang about teatime Kit did not trouble to disguise her tear-stained face with make-up before she answered it. Maggie had already seen the ravages, and would not be surprised.

'Hello, Ma...'

Her voice choked back into her throat. Brook, not Maggie, stood on the mat outside, but only for an instant. Before Kit had time to recover her wits, he was in the hall, kicking the door shut behind him with a well-aimed heel, and folding Kit in his arms with one co-ordinated movement.

'Kit...oh, *Kit*!' he muttered hoarsely. His kisses covered her tear-swollen eyes, asked forgiveness from their puffed lids. 'I couldn't keep away,' he groaned. 'I know you must hate me, and all my name stands for, but I had to come.'

'Hate *you*?' Kit felt as if the world was suddenly standing on its head. 'Why should I hate you? It wasn't your fault, any more than it was mine. It was Paul, and Fleur.'

'I thought you'd hate me because of what Fleur did to your marriage.'

'I thought you would hate me, because of what Paul did. That was why I didn't dare tell you...'

'Oh, my poor darling.' With tender fingers Brook tipped up Kit's face, the better to meet his lips. 'Your husband must have been putty in Fleur's hands. He wasn't her first affair. I found that out afterwards. There had been others, several of them, while I had to be away on business, which was why I divorced her.'

'Fleur wasn't Paul's first affair either. I found that out afterwards, too.'

'Forget them both. They aren't worth our thoughts. Although I suppose, in an odd sort of way, we ought to be grateful to them, because they brought us together.'

'I thought it was my Metro that brought us together.' Kit dimpled suddenly as a small ember of happiness inside her began to burn more brightly, warming away the tension.

'That was fate. You can't deny the pattern fits. We're meant for each other, Kit. You saw it at the carnival. You stopped fighting me then, and your whole attitude towards me changed, until the man at the harbour office called me by name. It wasn't until after I left you last night that I realised that must be the reason why you changed. I'd searched and searched in my mind to remember if it was anything I'd done to upset you. I thought I was losing my reason, but this morning I came to my senses. It had been staring me in the face all the time, and I was too blind to see. So I came back to you,' he said humbly, and Kit confessed,

'I didn't know what your surname was until then. You didn't tell me when we first met, and

Lois introduced you only as Brook. I assumed your second name must be Manning, the same as that of your uncle.'

'No, it's just . . .'

' . . . plain Galloway,' Kit chorused with a shaky laugh, and melted into his arms.

Timeless minutes later—minutes that restored Brook's colour to normal, and brought a rosy glow to Kit's cheeks and a brightness to her eyes which the man vowed silently should never be dimmed again—he said gravely, 'I couldn't get you out of my mind, after that first day in the restaurant. Your face haunted me.'

'It didn't stop you from leaving me at the end of the street, and letting me struggle with my portfolio on my own as far as the publisher's door,' Kit remembered with mock indignation.

'I went because I had to.'

'You had an appointment at Claridge's.'

'I skipped the appointment. I sent the shipping agent to deal with it instead. The deal was a big one, but my mind was in such a muddle after being with you, I couldn't think straight. All I could think about was you.'

So his appointment had not been with a woman after all, a woman of his own kind, rich and probably beautiful . . . Startled, Kit slapped down the strange, green-eyed sprite which she had not known existed inside her until now, and she listened with the sympathy of fellow-feeling as Brook confessed, 'I fought my feelings like mad. After Fleur, I was determined never to get caught up in love again.'

'I felt just the same, after Paul.'

'I lost the fight,' Brook confessed, and asked anxiously, 'What about you?'

'I lost it even before the carnival.'

'We've won each other,' Brook said contentedly. 'And our love will last. We'll still be holding hands on our golden wedding anniversary.'

'Our diamond anniversary,' Kit contradicted, and Brook's smile broadened.

'If we're still going to be spritely enough to hold hands on our diamond anniversary, we'll have to get married soon. Make it *very* soon, Kit,' he begged. 'We've wasted so much precious time.'

'Too much,' Kit agreed with a tremulous smile, 'but we'll have to have time to let our people know—my parents, and Alton and his wife.'

'Alton already knows.'

Kit gasped. 'How can he? I didn't know myself until . . .'

'I think he guessed when I twisted his arm to let me borrow his limo in return for the loan of my Jaguar. Anyway, he wished us both luck.'

Kit laughed. 'His wish has come true.'

'And mine.' Brook's lips were hungry on her own, but smiling too. 'I think Lois guessed which way the wind was blowing, because the day I left she offered me the loan of their house any time I wanted, she said, for a holiday. But she's never done that before.'

'She's a very shrewd woman, as well as a kind one.'

'Shall we take her up on her offer, then? We could use the *Dolphin* for transport.'

'It sounds fabulous,' Kit breathed contentedly. 'I still can't believe it's all worked out for us.'

'Will a celebration dinner tonight convince you?'

'I daren't come out looking like this,' Kit panicked. 'My face is all puffy with crying.'

'I'll spend my life making sure you never cry like that again,' Brook kissed away the ravages, and assured her.

'I know of a place where there are soft lights, and secluded tables, where no one will see.'

'Give me a minute or two to slip into something nice,' Kit capitulated, and Brook released her reluctantly.

'While you change, I'll phone the restaurant.'

Through the bedroom door Kit heard Brook dial a number, and then his deep voice carried through to her, 'A booking for eight o'clock, please. Yes, that will be fine. A table for two.'

A table for two...

Suddenly the warmth inside Kit burst into a steady flame that she knew would never again be extinguished. Brook was her tomorrow's man, for all of her tomorrows, and nothing would ever have the power to alter that.

'How do I look?' Short minutes later, she presented herself, and Brook's eyes glowed as he looked at her, catching sight of the dolphin pendant that rested against the soft silk of her dress, matching his cuff-links.

'You look perfect,' he said huskily. 'How do you feel?'

'Humming-bird happy,' Kit laughed, and ran into his waiting arms.

# Next Month's Romances

Each month you can choose from a wide variety of romance with Mills & Boon. Below are the new titles to look out for next month, why not ask either Mills & Boon Reader Service or your Newsagent to reserve you a copy of the titles you want to buy – just tick the titles you would like and either post to Reader Service or take it to any Newsagent and ask them to order your books.

| *Please save me the following titles:* | Please tick | √ |
|---|---|---|
| DAWN SONG | Sara Craven | |
| FALLING IN LOVE | Charlotte Lamb | |
| MISTRESS OF DECEPTION | Miranda Lee | |
| POWERFUL STRANGER | Patricia Wilson | |
| SAVAGE DESTINY | Amanda Browning | |
| WEST OF BOHEMIA | Jessica Steele | |
| A HEARTLESS MARRIAGE | Helen Brooks | |
| ROSES IN THE NIGHT | Kay Gregory | |
| LADY BE MINE | Catherine Spencer | |
| SICILIAN SPRING | Sally Wentworth | |
| A SCANDALOUS AFFAIR | Stephanie Howard | |
| FLIGHT OF FANTASY | Valerie Parv | |
| RISK TO LOVE | Lynn Jacobs | |
| DARK DECEIVER | Alex Ryder | |
| SONG OF THE LORELEI | Lucy Gordon | |
| A TASTE OF HEAVEN | Carol Grace | |

If you would like to order these books in addition to your regular subscription from Mills & Boon Reader Service please send £1.80 per title to: Mills & Boon Reader Service, Freepost, P.O. Box 236, Croydon, Surrey, CR9 9EL, quote your Subscriber No:.................................. (If applicable) and complete the name and address details below. Alternatively, these books are available from many local Newsagents including W.H.Smith, J.Menzies, Martins and other paperback stockists from 3 December 1993.

Name:.......................................................................................
Address:....................................................................................
..........................................................Post Code:........................

**To Retailer: If you would like to stock M&B books please contact your regular book/magazine wholesaler for details.**

You may be mailed with offers from other reputable companies as a result of this application. If you would rather not take advantage of these opportunities please tick box ☐